P9-EEI-847

Praise for Abby Gaines

"Gaines has a real talent for sparkling dialogue."
—*RT Book Reviews* on *Her So-Called Fiancé*

"Gaines tackles the complexities of family relationships
head-on in this entertaining read
filled with three-dimensional characters
you'll be rooting for until the very end."
—*RT Book Reviews* on *The Comeback*

"She knows how to weave
a wonderfully romantic tale together."
—*Fresh Fiction* on *The Groom Came Back*

"[An] emotional and compelling tale."
—*RT Book Reviews* on *Teaming Up*

Praise for Marisa Carroll

"These ladies know their racing
and seem to know their romance, too."
—*MotorSportsNews.net*

"[A] powerful, riveting family drama
with deftly drawn characters."
—*RT Book Reviews* on *Before Thanksgiving Comes*

"[A] fine tale of love
between two wonderful lead players."
—*Genre Go Round* on *Forbidden Attraction*

ROMANCE

OCT 2 2 2010

ABBY GAINES

Like some of her favorite NASCAR drivers, Abby Gaines's first love was open-wheel dirt-track racing. As editor of a speedway magazine, she spent many summer evenings at her favorite local track. But the lure of NASCAR—the speed, the power, the awesome scale—proved irresistible, just as it did for those drivers. Now, Abby's thrilled to combine her love of NASCAR with her love of writing.

As well as the NASCAR-licensed Harlequin series, Abby also writes novels for the Harlequin Superromance line. She lives with her husband and three children, a labradoodle and a cat who likes to walk the dog.

Visit Abby at www.abbygaines.com to read some NASCAR-themed short stories, or feel free to e-mail her, abby@abbygaines.com, and let her know if you enjoyed this story.

MARISA CARROLL

is the pen name of sisters Carol Wagner and Marian Franz. The team has been writing bestselling books for almost twenty-five years. During that time they have published more than forty titles, many for the Harlequin Superromance and NASCAR lines. They are the recipients of several industry awards, including a Lifetime Achievement Award from *RT Book Reviews* and a RITA® Award nomination from Romance Writers of America, and their books have been featured on the *USA TODAY,* Waldenbooks and B. Dalton bestseller lists. The sisters live near each other in northwestern Ohio, surrounded by children, grandchildren, brothers, sisters, aunts, uncles, cousins and old and dear friends.

NASCAR®

One in a Million

Abby Gaines 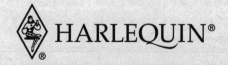 Marisa Carroll

HARLEQUIN®

TORONTO • NEW YORK • LONDON
AMSTERDAM • PARIS • SYDNEY • HAMBURG
STOCKHOLM • ATHENS • TOKYO • MILAN • MADRID
PRAGUE • WARSAW • BUDAPEST • AUCKLAND

If you purchased this book without a cover you should be aware that this book is stolen property. It was reported as "unsold and destroyed" to the publisher, and neither the author nor the publisher has received any payment for this "stripped book."

ISBN-13: 978-0-373-18540-5

ONE IN A MILLION

Copyright © 2010 by Harlequin Books S.A.

The publisher acknowledges the
copyright holders of the individual works
as follows:

NO ORDINARY MAN
Copyright © 2010 by Harlequin Books S.A.
Abby Gaines is acknowledged as the author of
"No Ordinary Man."

DAISY CHAIN
Copyright © 2010 by Harlequin Books S.A.
Marisa Carroll is acknowledged as the author of "Daisy Chain."

Recycling programs
for this product may
not exist in your area.

NASCAR® and the NASCAR Library Collection® are registered trademarks of the National Association for Stock Car Auto Racing, Inc.

All rights reserved. Except for use in any review, the reproduction or utilization of this work in whole or in part in any form by any electronic, mechanical or other means, now known or hereafter invented, including xerography, photocopying and recording, or in any information storage or retrieval system, is forbidden without the written permission of the publisher, Harlequin Enterprises Limited, 225 Duncan Mill Road, Don Mills, Ontario, Canada M3B 3K9.

This is a work of fiction. Names, characters, places and incidents are either the product of the author's imagination or are used fictitiously, and any resemblance to actual persons, living or dead, business establishments, events or locales is entirely coincidental.

This edition published by arrangement with Harlequin Books S.A.

For questions and comments about the quality of this book
please contact us at Customer_eCare@Harlequin.ca

® and TM are trademarks of the publisher. Trademarks indicated with ® are registered in the United States Patent and Trademark Office, the Canadian Trade Marks Office and in other countries.

www.eHarlequin.com

Printed in U.S.A.

CONTENTS

An excerpt from Hilton Branch's prison journal…

I managed to get word to my children, but they refuse to see me. I shouldn't be surprised, I know. They've made their contempt clear.

Damn it, they hurt me. I know, I know—I hurt them first.

But they don't understand. This isn't about my pride or asking them to love me again. I don't want to dig up the past, and I've already asked for the forgiveness they refuse to grant me. This is about survival. About family they don't know they have.

Lily, sweet, angelic Lily with that rosebud mouth always ready to grin at me, her chubby little arms reaching for me, closing around my neck and laying her head on my shoulders.

She makes me feel ten feet tall. How delighted she is to see me, how she cuddles into me, listens raptly to my silliest story as though I were spouting pearls of wisdom.

Why did I never have time for my first four when they were small?

I was making a living for them, I told myself. Meeting the standards Maeve's family expected for her, Texas royalty that she is. Her father made it clear to me that the price of gaining access to their privileged world was that Maeve should never be disappointed, never have to emerge from that ivory tower in which he'd placed his little girl.

I took that bank of his, and I made it more than he ever dreamed it could be. I created an empire, and I had the respect and admiration of high rollers all over this country.

But there was a price, and I never knew it. Not until Rose.

They'll take the news hard, my first family, and it's not fair. She's the innocent—they can't hate her, though they will want to. Even if they do, they have to help me save her. Amelia, too, even though she isn't mine. Doesn't matter—she belongs to Rose, and Rose is special. And Lily, little Lily...

I want to rage, to howl. Hit something. I can't stand sitting here, rotting here with no money, no power, no way to fight back while those thugs at Biscayne Bay threaten everything I love.

Maeve. She's the answer. She forgave me already—said she was done with me, but she'll fight like a tiger for her children. She always did. Penny and Will have children of their own now—surely they'll understand that nothing else matters.

Begging sticks in my throat, but pride is not the issue anymore. My pride has cost all of us too much already.

I can bear my children's contempt—I've earned it.

What I can't bear is to lose a single one of them.

I have to make them listen.

No Ordinary Man

Abby Gaines

For Mum—no ordinary woman.
With love always.

CHAPTER ONE

SEIZE THE DAY. ELI Ward knew there were some fancy Latin words for the motto he'd adopted back when he was a kid, but the plain English version had always fired him up just fine. This weekend's NASCAR Sprint Cup Series race in Bristol, Tennessee, would be no different. *Seize the Day. Win the race.*

Generally he preferred to do his seizing, and his winning, on more than two hours' sleep, but if that was all he'd had…

Eli bit down on a yawn as he crossed the stretch of grass in front of the motor home belonging to Gil Sizemore, owner of Double S Racing. His boss.

Gil's phone call, and his impatient demand for a meeting *right now,* had forced Eli to roll out of bed a couple of hours earlier than planned. Result: eyes pinker than a scared bunny's, a killer thirst and a fog around his brain that he hoped would clear up any second.

A couple of kids rounded the side of a nearby motor home and dodged past him, shrieking at full volume. The headache drilling a hole in Eli's forehead mined a new seam of pain.

He slipped his sunglasses on as he knocked on Gil's door. He'd been in such a rush to get here, now was the first chance he'd had to wonder what this meeting was about. Gil had sure sounded cranky.

Eli was surprised to find himself wishing he hadn't spun out in the closing laps of last weekend's race at Michigan.

Surprised because he didn't waste time on regrets. He couldn't change that piece of history, any more than he could change the other sucky results he'd delivered over the past couple of months. You had to move on.

The motor home door opened. Quinn Parrish, founder of Rev Energy Drinks and Eli's biggest sponsor, stared down at him. Gil hadn't mentioned Quinn was in on this meeting.

"Come in." Quinn jerked his head toward the interior.

Eli stepped up, eliminating most of the height difference. Gil's motor home was one of the nicer ones around. Plushly restrained, like the man himself. Built-in black leather sofas lined both sides of the navy blue-carpeted living area. A matching swivel armchair backed a desk. Model stock cars filled a display case on the opposite wall, but Eli knew better than to think Gil Sizemore played games. His boss sat on the far sofa, arms folded across his chest. At around forty years old Gil might be one of the youngest team owners in NASCAR, but he commanded respect in every quarter.

Eli caught a strong whiff of trouble emanating from Gil's and Quinn's matching stony faces. Between them, these two men held his future in their hands. Suddenly it felt as if they had him at a disadvantage.

He shook off the moment of uncertainty. He was a great driver and they knew it. "Good morning, gentlemen." He shook hands all around, then settled into the armchair.

The hot seat?

Eli grasped the initiative, just as he liked to out on the race track. "Quinn, I haven't seen you since last weekend, and I'd like to apologize for letting Rev down. I thought I'd nailed a top-five finish, but I underestimated Jeb Stallworth's willingness to risk a smash. He pulled it off, I didn't. I'm sorry."

Few people could resist a genuine apology, and Eli meant every word.

Quinn grunted.

"Take off those sunglasses," Gil ordered.

Rats. Eli shoved the shades up onto his head and tried not to wince against the glare of the August sunshine slicing through the vertical blinds behind his boss.

"Late night?" Gil asked.

Which was *not* a guess based on the state of Eli's eyes. Eli would bet Gil's informant was his nephew Marcus, a rookie in the NASCAR Camping World Truck Series. The guy who wanted Eli's job.

"If I'd known about this morning's meeting, I'd have come home earlier," Eli said shortly. He was twenty-eight years old, he didn't have to account for his every move.

"You left The Corral after 5:00 a.m.," Gil said.

"And Marcus knows this because, what, he was out for an early morning run?" Eli should have had the eighteen-year-old thrown out of the nightclub, but he'd figured Gil wouldn't appreciate a fake ID scandal. Besides, he was young enough to remember the thrill of crashing a club underage. He'd kept an eye on Marcus without realizing the brat was returning the favor.

"Marcus didn't have a 7:00 a.m. appointment with a personal trainer paid for by this team," Gil snapped.

Damn. "I'll call Jodie to apologize."

Gil continued, "Nor did my nephew overturn a table full of drinks—"

"I was ducking a punch," Eli protested. "You don't like drivers getting into fights." It'd been damn hard not to sock the guy right back. Eli could never figure why some men had to prove their machismo by lashing out at anyone richer or more successful than they were.

"Look, Gil, I admit it was a late night. But I was on my

own time and I met this girl—" he caught the roll of Gil's eyes but he carried on "—it was her twenty-first birthday and her family lives in Australia. She was depressed because she had no one to celebrate with…"

"Don't try and tell me your mindless partying was an act of charity," Gil roared.

Hell. Gil never lost his temper. What was going on?

Whatever it was, Eli suspected his explanation—the girl had gone overboard on her first legal night of drinking, so he'd stuck around until she agreed to go home in a cab—wouldn't cut any ice.

Besides, she'd been a lot of fun and he'd had a darned good time, so he couldn't exactly stake a claim to sainthood.

"Being a NASCAR driver is a job, not a hobby to fill the hours between parties," Quinn said.

Eli knuckled his forehead. "I know that." He needed water, but now wasn't the right time to get up and pour himself a glass from the bottle on the counter.

"Which means you don't get to turn up just when it suits you." Quinn stretched out his legs and eyed his expensively casual shoes as if they could grant him insight into Eli's behavior. "Of course, you're the driver and I'm only the sponsor." His tone was ironic, but Eli knew better than to smile. "But I figure that when you drive the way you have the past month, Eli, you don't go out with one girl after another. You stay in, and you fix whatever the hell is messing with you on the track."

Quinn had made millions from Rev Energy Drinks. The old-fashioned way, not by relying on his caffeine-infused product for energy. He'd slogged through years of setbacks before making it big.

Lucky for Eli, racing had always come easy. Until recently.

"Should we be talking to Kevin about the car?" Gil asked. Kevin Horton was Eli's crew chief.

"The car's fine, Kevin's doing a great job," Eli assured him.

"So the problem is the driver." Gil stated the obvious. Then one side of his mouth softened. "Eli, if you're having personal issues, Quinn can leave right now and we can talk. Hash it out."

Eli recoiled. "I'm fine, Gil, but thanks." In his nearly two years at Double S, Gil had never tried to force a personal conversation on him. Maybe he'd been here too long, maybe he was in a rut.

Gil's mouth returned to its hard line. "In that case, I need to lay down the law."

Uh-oh.

"If your attitude to race preparation doesn't improve, starting today, your future at Double S will be severely limited."

The sudden sick feeling in Eli's stomach had to be hangover-related. No way would Gil fire him. And if he did, there were other teams, other cars. Eli's entire life was proof there's always another opportunity out there. No need to worry.

"You can't fault my attitude on the track, and that's what matters," he pointed out.

"You need to make the Chase," Gil said flatly.

Now *that,* Eli wouldn't argue with. The top twelve drivers, based on series points after the race at Richmond in four weeks' time, would qualify to compete in the Chase for the NASCAR Sprint Cup. They would go into the last ten races of the season with their points reset at a level the other drivers couldn't match. Which meant only those twelve had a chance to win the overall NASCAR Sprint Cup Series championship for the year.

Eli was currently eighteenth in series points. He could still make the Chase…if his results improved. Fast.

"The Chase is my number one priority," he assured the other men.

"You need focus," Gil told him. Gentleman Gil's favorite F-word. To listen to him, you'd think every disaster could be averted, every problem solved, with just a little more focus.

Eli's approach to life was simpler. You played the hand you were dealt as best you could. And when it didn't pan out, you folded and moved on to the next round.

Still, he nodded in response to Gil's homily. It wouldn't hurt to focus some more these next few weeks.

"No more nightclubs between now and Richmond," Gil elaborated.

"Hey!" Eli protested. "That's how I relax. I'm no use to the team all wound-up."

"I don't like to set limits on your personal life, but you don't have anyone else advising you on these things." Other times, Gil joked that Eli was lucky not to have family to interfere. His own family was always poking their noses into his life, albeit in the nicest, slightly bemused way.

"Then there's the girlfriends," Gil said. "I'm sick of the parade of one-minute wonders through my garage. Get rid of them. Why not stick with just one—get yourself a steady girlfriend."

Quinn must have seen Eli's horror. He looked as if he was stifling a smile. "Cheer up, Eli. You might find it refreshing not to date a different woman every week."

Yeah, right.

"No more serial dating, got it," Eli said. Because he had no choice, not because who he dated was any of his boss's business, or his sponsor's. One of the best things about being an instantly recognizable NASCAR Sprint Cup Series driver was that women found him attractive and, like him, had no illusions about a relationship lasting. Everyone had a good time.

Gil looked relieved to have his way.

Eli seized the opportunity to dig for some wiggle room. "But, guys, there are no guarantees in NASCAR. I'll put more focus into my driving, but I can't promise I'll make the Chase."

Quinn looked amused. "Here's a guarantee for you. If you don't make the Chase, Rev will pull its sponsorship at the end of this season."

Eli's heart lurched, then thudded double-time. Gil didn't look surprised at the threat; he'd obviously had this conversation with Quinn already. Probably over coffee at six this morning, as Eli was staggering to bed.

No wonder Gil's nerves were frayed. Were he and Quinn in cahoots, playing good cop, bad cop to make Eli toe their line?

"I have another guarantee." Gil's gravelly voice cut through Eli's thoughts. "If you don't make the Chase, if you lose us a twelve million dollar sponsorship, you'll be out of that car. I'll give the ride to someone else."

Not good cop, bad cop.

Bad cop, worse cop.

"Do I make myself clear?" Gil switched into the Charleston-patrician mode that created a distance between him and whoever incurred his disapproval.

"Clear," Eli agreed, dryness turning his mouth into a dustbowl.

He needed sleep.

He needed water.

He needed a miracle.

CHAPTER TWO

TWO HOURS LATER, the sun had gone and a misty drizzle hung in the air. As Eli crossed from the hauler to the garage, he tried to revel in the smell of damp, warm pavement, in the babble of excited fans, in the clash of music blaring from the infield and merchandise offers echoing over the PA system.

But Gil's threat to take away the only thing that mattered had sucked all the joy out of the weekend.

In the garage, his team was putting the final touches to the No. 502 car before his practice. A lot of drivers were superstitious about green cars, but Eli never felt anything but lucky behind the wheel of his green-gold-and-white beauty.

If I could get Gil off my back, I'd find my groove again.

"Hey, Eli." One of the guys clustered around the car hailed him.

Eli plastered on the ready smile they expected. His team liked that nothing got him down, unlike some drivers who let their bad mood pervade the whole operation.

Eli might not be the most reliable guy in the world when it came to dating or early nights. But when it came to facing life's problems with a grin and a shrug, he was a shoo-in.

Kevin Horton, his crew chief, was reading the No. 502 car's setup details on his PC screen with a critical eye. "We'll look at putting in a round of wedge after we see how you go in those turns," he told Eli.

"Great. The guys had the car in beautiful shape yesterday."

Kevin nodded approval of Eli's sharing the credit for his eighth-place qualifying. Qualifying well wasn't his problem. The problem was the dozen or so places he'd been losing during the races...when he even finished.

Farther down the garage, Eli saw Dixon Rogers, owner of Fulcrum Racing. Fulcrum was the gold standard, the team Eli had longed to drive for ever since he started racing. Top of the list of teams he planned to approach for a new job, starting Monday. If Gil didn't want him, Eli wasn't about to hang around at Double S. Maybe he should have a word with Dixon now....

Kevin flipped the laptop closed. He glanced over Eli's shoulder. "Your fan club's arrived."

Eli heard the clatter of high heels on concrete, the breathy giggles and whispered speculation ("Is that really *him?*"). Women. He fought the urge to turn around. A driver in a NASCAR garage forbidden to flirt was like a dieter trapped in a candy store.

"Nice blonde in a tight red T-shirt." Kevin never failed to spot the talent. "Too bad she's not here for me."

"Too bad she's off-limits for me," Eli muttered.

"Looks mighty interested, too," Kevin commented with a distinct lack of sympathy.

"Maybe one date wouldn't hurt," Eli said.

"You wanna ask Gil?" Obviously his crew chief knew about Gil's ultimatum.

Eli sighed. "I'll head to the hauler, avoid temptation."

He turned, and immediately spotted the blonde in the red T-shirt. She was a knockout, with a great smile. He had to walk right by her and her friends; it would be rude to ignore them.

"Hi, ladies." His gaze lingered on the blonde.

She lowered her lashes in a flirty way. "Hey, Eli, think you can beat Linc out there tomorrow?"

Ha, a question about his job! He had a right, a *duty,* to answer. He took a moment to explain exactly why he would literally run rings around his teammate Linc Shepherd in tomorrow's race, which led to more questions from her and her friends, all charming women. Even if they did press so close it was difficult to get away. The volume went up as they chatted.

He wasn't dumb, he knew they found him especially charming and amusing because of the uniform he wore. He didn't have a problem with that; a guy would be nuts not to enjoy their company. He responded to their requests for autographs, scrawling his signature across programs, notebooks, even one woman's wrist.

"Buy you a drink later?" the blonde asked. "There's a country music bar in town."

His instinctive response was to say, *Sure.* He needed to take his mind off his worries. And he liked the blonde, liked her wide smile and her sassy tone.

He glanced up, and saw Gil in the garage entrance. Watching with unconcealed irritation. At the same moment, someone grabbed Eli's arm and tugged, which was overstepping the boundary.

He had to lower his gaze to find the culprit: a slight woman, a girl really—she looked about eighteen with a track-logoed ball cap jammed on her head.

"Excuse me," he said coolly, with a pointed stare at her hand, still on his arm.

"Oh, thank goodness," she said.

"Uh, excuse me?" he said again, confused now.

"I've been trying to get your attention for the past two minutes. I have a message for you."

That old chestnut. Eli would've smiled if he hadn't been

conscious of Gil's disapproval. The first few occasions he'd heard that line, he'd fallen for it. Even let a woman into his motor home once, on the mistaken assumption that if she'd found her way into the lot she must be legit.

"Tell it to my secretary," he advised his newest admirer.

The blonde in the red T-shirt giggled.

To Eli's annoyance, Ball Cap Girl didn't let go. "You think I'm a fan? One of *them?*" she asked, astonished, lifting her chin toward the other women.

Now that she mentioned it…she was like a sparrow among swans in her loose-fitting light gray and black shirt, again bearing the track logo, and her dark pants. She stood too close for Eli to see her feet, but anyone that short must be wearing sneakers, not heels.

"Mr. Ward, I work here," she explained. "Souvenir shop assistant, track tour guide and race-weekend gofer. The message is from Bob Coffman."

Coffman was the president of the track here at Bristol. Eli registered the name badge pinned to her chest. *Jennifer*. The colorless clothing must be her uniform.

"Bob's a great guy," Eli said.

Her mouth, which had been pursed with anxiety, relaxed. Turned out she had nice-shaped lips. "He's a wonderful boss," she agreed as she released his arm. "If we could just step aside from your, uh, friends for a moment, I'll pass on the message."

With the conversation taking an unfamiliar turn, the other women eased back; now was the time to make a break for the hauler.

"Walk with me," Eli ordered Jennifer.

Her eyebrows, darker than the brown hair peeking out from beneath her ball cap, drew together over her petite nose in distress. "I'm sorry, Mr. Ward, I didn't make myself clear. When I said I'm a race-weekend gofer, I meant for *Bob*. I'm very busy."

"And I'm going this way, so if you want me to hear that message…" Eli grasped her elbow and maneuvered the two of them through the crowd of fans, who parted obligingly.

Despite the noise around him, he heard Jennifer's hiss of alarm.

"We're only going to the hauler," he reassured her, amused. She obviously took her gofering seriously.

Outside, the drizzle had stopped and sunlight had broken through the gray cloud, piercing in its brilliance. More women converged on Eli, but when they saw him with the track girl—Jennifer—they fell back.

With Eli ignoring Jennifer's protests about how busy she was, they made it to the hauler in record time. Someone should tell her that slow Tennessee drawl wasn't about to hold up a NASCAR Sprint Cup Series driver. It might, on the other hand, warm up a cup of coffee…

Where did that come from? Eli gave his head a sharp shake. They'd reached the hauler; the automatic door swished open, then closed behind them, cocooning them in silence.

"Okay," Eli said, still disconcerted by that coffee thought, "I'm Eli Ward, hi." Duh. Not one of his smoothest lines. He stuck out a hand.

She didn't notice because she was too busy rubbing her elbow where he'd held her—he was certain he hadn't hurt her—and darting little glances around the hauler, her expression a mix of curious and…hunted?

"Nice to meet you, too," he quipped in the face of her lack of response. "Let me guess, you're Jennifer."

She fingered her name badge. "Just Jen."

The badge perched on the kind of sweet curve not even a shapeless uniform could hide. Eli leaned against the counter, folded his arms across his chest and shot her the intimate smile his female fans adored. "Okay, Just Jen, what does Bob want to tell me?"

This urge to flirt with a sparrow had to be a kneejerk rebellion against Gil's "no women" stipulation.

The sparrow didn't flirt back.

Sure, Jennifer's eyes—brown, unexpectedly light—widened at the sensual vibes he was sending her way. Then she laced her fingers in front of her, like a nun about to pray. "Mr. Ward," she said sternly, "there are two women in Bob's office. Both from around here, both in varying states of hysteria, both claiming to be your girlfriend."

Eli pinched the bridge of his nose. Wouldn't Gil love to hear that? "They're not my girlfriends."

"But one of them—"

"End of story," Eli said, struggling to keep his tone light on what was fast turning into the worst day of his life. "Tell Bob to call security."

Jennifer pursed her nice-shaped lips and didn't move. "One of them says she's having your baby."

CHAPTER THREE

JEN WAS SUDDENLY inclined to believe the pretty, pregnant redhead whose eyes had shone with tears as she talked about her struggle to provide for her unborn child.

All week, Jen's female colleagues had been cooing about the gorgeous NASCAR drivers about to descend on their little track. None of the names were familiar to Jen, who hadn't worked here long enough to see a NASCAR race, but one name had received way more than its fair share of cooing: Eli Ward. Who, if you believed Tracy in accounting, was the sexiest man alive. And who, according to Janelle on reception, had broken more hearts than should be legal.

Jen had taken the gossip with a grain of salt, and continued to reserve judgment through the arrival of the two alleged girlfriends in Bob's office. Bob had warned her not to be sucked in by what might be elaborate ploys to get Eli's attention.

But meeting Eli Ward in the flesh lent a whole new weight to everything she'd heard.

Tracy in accounting was right: Jen had never seen such a good-looking man. It looked as if Janelle was right about the broken hearts, too, given how Eli had been lapping up the admiration of the women in the garage. Admiration that was purely about his looks. According to Caleb in maintenance, Eli wasn't even a good race car driver, always making careless mistakes.

Everything about him shrieked *unreliable*.

But the most shocking thing of all…when Eli's fingers had curled around Jen's elbow, every nerve ending in her body had converged on that point, leaving the rest of her feeling rubbery, numb. She'd let him lead her to the hauler like a particularly stupid lamb might follow a wolf in sheep's clothing.

Jen would never, in a million years, have imagined she would be so shallow.

It was most unsettling.

I've been unsettled all day. From the moment she'd arrived at the track to find it transformed from local raceway to a NASCAR mini-city, powered by a buzz of excitement, all five of her senses had been overwhelmed. Then somehow Eli Ward—with his shaggy blond hair and too-green eyes and devil-may-care grin—had tapped into some mysterious *other* sense.

She was so busy trying, and failing, to excuse her body's extreme response to his touch, she almost missed his reaction to the pregnancy claim. Fleetingly his face paled, his lips formed an unspoken curse-word. Then his pallor receded and he shook out his fingers, as if discarding the redhead's allegation.

"The lady might be pregnant," he drawled, "but not by me."

The steel beneath the lazy tone was clearly intended to nix further argument. But if he was as careless in his relationships as Caleb said he was on the track… That poor girl's baby needed a father. Jen squared her shoulders. "She seems quite categorical about your, uh, role in the proceedings and the, uh, consequence. Maybe you should come see her, just to be sure?"

His smile was relaxed, but the gaze that settled on her was emerald-hard. "I missed the spring race here due to injury, which means I haven't been in the area for a year." He scratched the back of his head. "Remind me, how long does it take for a baby to grow after a man and a woman…?"

Heat, stupid and naive, climbed Jen's cheeks. Pathetic, after the explicit speculation she'd listened to in the office all week without blushing. But something about Eli even *hinting* at sex… She wrapped her arms around her middle and forced herself to sound calm. "I'm sure you don't need me to explain the facts of life, Mr. Ward."

She was one hundred percent certain that he possessed far more of those facts than she did.

"You sound like one of my ninth grade English teachers," Eli said appreciatively.

"*One* of them? You were expelled?" Her newly lurid mind envisaged all kinds of inappropriate behavior. Good grief, how did he have this effect on her? "I'm sorry," she said quickly, "it's none of my business."

Unexpectedly one side of his mouth kicked up. "You're not related to Gil Sizemore, are you? Did he send you to spy on me?"

Jen didn't know much about NASCAR, but she did know Gil Sizemore was Eli's team owner. "No," she said. Why on earth would Mr. Sizemore want to spy on his own driver?

"Phew." Eli thumped a fist to his chest. "You had me worried. That puritanical streak of yours has a real Sizemore flavor."

Guilt nudged her. Much as she loved the grandparents who'd raised her, she tried not to indulge in their habit of assuming the worst of everyone. "I'm sorry," she said again. "I was just worried about the lady in Bob's office, and I'm sure you'd agree that even with the best of protection, accidents can happen." *Aargh! Now I'm lecturing him about contraception.*

Jen clamped her lips tight before she blurted something even more tactless.

Those hypnotic green eyes sparkled. Surely that wasn't his natural eye color?

"I hope not," Eli said.

She parted her lips just enough to say, "Excuse me?"

"You said accidents happen. I can't afford another crash this weekend."

Grateful that he'd let her off the hook, she said sympathetically, "I heard you're not doing too well."

When Eli gaped, she realized she'd misspoken again.

"I can't decide if your bluntness is refreshing, or just blunt," he said. "Are you always this…honest?"

"It's the best policy," she said seriously. "Though I try not to cause offence."

He chuckled. His gaze roamed her face. "Even your skin looks honest."

"I—skin can't look honest!" She grabbed hold of the counter, her fingers fumbling against a socket set. He was doing it again, turning her topsy-turvy. Her skin, her *body,* prickled all over. And he knew it, judging by the laughter in his eyes. She was hopelessly out of her depth. "Mr. Ward," she said firmly, "I don't appreciate being made fun of. And in the unlikely event you meant that as a compliment, I should warn you I'm not about to fall at your feet."

His grin widened. He looked so vital her heart actually stopped for a fraction of a second.

"Now that's a shame, because my team keeps this floor real clean." He nodded at the serviceable beige linoleum running the length of the hauler. "If you did want to do any falling, I can assure you there'd be no, uh, hygiene *consequence.*"

He was employing the same kind of stilted language she'd used talking about his supposedly pregnant girlfriend. His eyes danced, mocking her lack of sophistication.

"I think we're done here," she said stiffly. "I'll deliver your message to Bob."

"Time we both got back to work," he agreed. "After all, I'm *not doing too well*." He echoed her again.

She colored. "If it's any consolation, those twelve women you were flirting with in the garage seemed quite impressed."

"More like eight," he said modestly. "But thanks."

"It wasn't a compliment."

"Jealous, chickadee?"

She didn't mean to snort, it just slipped out.

Eli guffawed. She had to give him credit for not taking offence. Jen found herself smiling wryly. Now that his face was completely relaxed, she realized he'd been tense before. Genuine amusement softened his mouth, made his lips look—

"I'm up here, chickadee," Eli said softly.

Jen jerked her gaze from his mouth. Her eyes met his.

There was a moment of crackling silence while they stared at each other. Heat suffused her. Then she blinked, long and hard, severing the contact.

Eli frowned. "How old are you?"

"Twenty-two." *Going on thirteen.* "Time I left," she said.

"Yeah. Bye, chickadee." Despite the teasing nickname, he sounded...remote.

"Drive safely," she said with sudden vehemence, imagining him caught up in another crash.

Eli tilted his head, his expression a blend of surprise and amusement. "You want to wish me luck, too? Because much as I want to finish in one piece, I mostly want to finish first."

"I don't really care about that," she admitted.

He shook his head. "You sure are the strangest race track employee I ever met."

He escorted her to the automatic door, which hissed open as they approached. Outside, a bunch of loitering women came to attention, craning their necks.

Jen thought she heard a faint groan from Eli. But a sidelong glance revealed he was smiling.

"Eli!" One of the fans waved a program at him. "Sign this!"

Immediately a clamor rose from the rest of the women.

Despite the flippancy that suggested he didn't care much about anything, Jen felt sorry for him. It couldn't be easy, putting a brave face on his poor driving performance.

Then his arm landed across her shoulders.

"So, Jen, do you want to spend tomorrow with my team?" he asked, loud enough for the fans to hear.

Disappointment rippled through the throng.

For one second, the wild possibility that Eli Ward was attracted to her ran rampant through Jen's head.

Twin sensations slammed her. Panic…and excitement. Which one was responsible for the way her brain clouded, her palms turned sweaty, her breath came faster?

"I can't," she said with absolute certainty.

Eli stepped closer, so close his eyes were brilliant. *He must wear colored contact lenses*….

"You understand I just asked you on a date, right?" he said, more quietly, so the fans couldn't listen in. "You'd spend tomorrow with me, up until the start of the race. Then watch the race in my pits."

Oh, yes, she understood all right. Not *why*, not at all, but certainly *what*.

Jen stepped back into the hauler, clear of the automatic door's attempts to close. A part of her wanted to shriek *Yes* in response to his invitation. "It's not possible," she managed.

He carried on blocking the door. "Are you married? En-gaged?" His eyes alighted on her bare left hand.

"No." She wrapped her right hand over her left.

"Seeing someone?"

She shook her head.

"Because you and I had a connection a moment ago," he said. "So I can't see why you'd refuse."

He'd felt it, too? "You and I…wouldn't work," she said, flustered.

"I wasn't asking you to marry me." He was trying not to smile, with limited success. How silly she must seem to him! "I just want a little company," he continued.

"Mr. Ward, there are dozens of women outside who'd jump at the chance to date you. Most of them prettier than I am, all of them less blunt, I'm sure. Why me?"

He shrugged. "Why not you? You make me laugh."

Jen hadn't heard many pickup lines in her life—in fact, she'd never been picked up by a stranger—but she was pretty sure *Why not you?* followed by an admission that he was laughing at her, wouldn't cut it with any self-respecting woman. Eli Ward had the sense of entitlement that came with celebrity.

"I'm ordinary." She'd decided long ago that she didn't do crazy things, that she wanted an ordinary life, with all the trimmings: ordinary job, ordinary home, ordinary man… "I'm not interested in dating a man like you."

I'm not, she told her protesting hormones sternly.

His expression turned quizzical. "I'm not *ordinary* enough for you?"

Okay, when he said it like that, it sounded weird.

"Some things just don't go together," she explained. "You're a lion, I'm a housecat. You're a peacock, I'm a duck."

"A sparrow," he corrected.

Ouch! "Whatever," she said tautly.

"Sparrows are much cuter than ducks." He reached out, tweaked a strand of hair that had escaped her cap.

A flood of lightness spread through her. "Mr. Ward, this conversation is—"

"Extraordinary?" he suggested.

She huffed a laugh. Which meant she let down her guard and found herself drowning in those eyes again. "I like ordinary guys, with regular jobs," she insisted, unfortunately breathless. "You drive a race car, you're larger than life with your long hair and your fake green eyes…"

"My *what?*"

"No one has eyes that green unless they're wearing colored contacts," she pointed out. "I know you have a…a sex-symbol image to uphold, but if you wanted them to look real, you should have chosen a more natural shade."

"A sex-symbol image?" Eli hooted with laughter, drawing stares from the women outside. "Talking to you, chickadee, is like driving a race car blindfolded."

She clutched at her throat. "Tell me you've never done that."

"Of course I haven't." He eyed her as if she was crazy. Then he smirked. "Funny you should say that stuff about a sex symbol…did you know I was labeled *Mr. Irresistible* in *Now Woman* magazine earlier this year?"

"I did not know that," she admitted.

"Does that make you want to spend tomorrow with me?"

She shook her head, not trusting her mouth to form the word *No.*

"I should've guessed you would have extraordinary powers of resistance," he mused.

Darn it, she wanted to laugh again. "Mr. Ward, I'm leaving."

"You called me a peacock, I called you a sparrow, I think that qualifies us for first name terms, don't you—" his smile turned knowing "—Jen?" He drew the syllable out, long and deep.

Jen sucked in a breath. "Goodbye, Mr.—Eli."

Her verbal stumble brought his gaze to her lips. "I think I'll come talk to Bob," he announced.

"Why?" she asked, alarmed. "There's no law against refusing to date you, is there?" Folk around here were so nuts about NASCAR, it wouldn't surprise her if she'd committed a cardinal sin.

"Don't you worry about a thing." Eli's affability only heightened her anxiety. "Lead on, chickadee."

"ELI, GOOD TO SEE YOU." Bob Coffman shook Eli's hand as he ushered him into his office. "You didn't need to come all the way over here. My head of security had the bright idea of offering the pregnant woman a DNA test, told her we could do it onsite. Not true, of course. But she left in a hurry and the other one followed soon after."

"They were lying?" Jen said, outraged. "Both of them?"

Bob and Eli regarded her indulgently.

"Occupational hazard," Eli said.

"That's terrible." Jen wheeled around to scan the reception area. If either of those women was still on the premises, she'd—

Eli put a hand on her shoulder, and the intention blurred, submerged by her awareness of him. "I'm over it, Jen, I don't care."

"You *should* care." She felt awful: she'd rushed to judge Eli on the basis of his reputation, when those women were the ones lacking in integrity.

"Unfortunately this kind of thing happens every so often," Bob said. "I'm sorry it happened at my track, Eli."

"Not your fault." Eli took a seat on the faded velour couch that was out of keeping with the rest of the black lacquered office furniture. "But I'm not above taking advantage of your embarrassment to ask a favor."

Bob looked perplexed, but he sat down behind his desk. "You can always ask."

"I'll get back to work," Jen said.

"Actually, could you stick around?" Eli asked.

She perched on the edge of the seat Bob indicated, ready to defend herself against charges of unlawfully refusing to date a NASCAR driver.

Eli leaned forward, hands clasped between his knees. "Bob, you're pretty clued in, so I figure you're aware of the challenge I'm facing."

What challenge? Finding a helmet big enough for his head? Jen eyed him. Even if his ego hadn't been massive, that shaggy blond hair must get in the way. His eyes met hers, their gleam suggesting he'd read her thoughts. Of course he hadn't! Still, she dropped her gaze to her sneakers—the sole was coming away from the left one, which wasn't surprising. She'd been wearing them for years.

"I am," Bob confirmed. "You and Gil can get through this, Eli, but it might not be easy."

"Not if any more pregnant girlfriends show up." Eli straightened. "That's why I'm asking you to lend me Jennifer tomorrow."

Jennifer's head snapped up. "*Lend* me? What am I, a ballpoint pen?"

Bob pressed his fingers into his desk and leaned back in his chair. "You'd better explain."

"I need someone to keep my fans—the female fans—at bay so I can focus on the race," Eli said.

"You want a bodyguard?" Jen asked.

His gaze flicked over her small frame so fast she couldn't

be sure, but it struck her he wasn't thinking *bodyguard*. Yet anything else was even more ludicrous, as she'd already made clear to him.

"Not a bodyguard," he said. "I want a girlfriend."

CHAPTER FOUR

A girlfriend?

Jen gripped the edge of her seat. This *was* about the fact she'd turned Eli down!

"The fans are important to me and the team," Eli told Bob. "I don't want to offend them when they get overenthusiastic. But I can't afford the distraction before a race."

Jen had seen that blonde in the skimpy red T-shirt practically rubbing herself against Eli, and he hadn't looked at all unhappy.

Bob glanced toward the enormous window overlooking the crowded stadium. "How does this fit with you dating Jennifer?"

"It doesn't," Jen said urgently.

"Pretend-dating," Eli clarified. "If I have a companion, the female fans will see me as off-limits."

That was why he'd asked her on a date? Because he wanted a decoy?

Jen bit her lip. It wasn't as if a girl like her would capture the attention of a guy like him for more than five minutes. But she was suddenly certain they would have been five *glorious* minutes, and she felt…cheated.

"Jen certainly wouldn't distract you from your racing," Bob agreed, unwittingly insulting. "She's a quiet little thing."

Eli turned that preposterously green gaze on her. "Now that I hadn't noticed."

She didn't believe he'd noticed anything about her at all. Any other woman to deliver Bob's message would have been invited to be his date for the race. Jen knew she wasn't anything special, but she deserved better!

"I wouldn't dare come between you and your fans," she said. "I'd be stomped by stilettos."

"You were ready to tackle those lying women on my behalf," Eli reminded her. "Jen, I guarantee you'll have a good time."

"I'm not here for a good time," she said primly.

"You could do with some fun, Jen," Bob inserted.

It dawned on her that in the past five minutes her boss had stated in several ways that he thought she was dull.

She wasn't dull, she was reliable. Which the last time she looked was a *good* quality.

"I have plenty of fun planned," she defended herself. It was true. She would have fun, just as soon as she secured her future, and Granddad's. Of course, it wouldn't be the kind of fun Eli was offering. High-octane, with an element of danger.

She liked her fun a whole lot safer.

"I don't see the problem," Eli said. "I need a girlfriend, you need some fun. Why not seize the day?" He winked conspiratorially.

She was ashamed that her stomach fluttered, that her hormones didn't have more self-respect. She'd always considered *Seize the Day* to be a license for irresponsibility, a belief reinforced by every warning her grandparents had drilled into her.

"Bob," Eli said, "this arrangement wouldn't work if you felt obliged to mention it to Gil."

"I don't discuss drivers' personal lives with anyone," Bob assured him.

They were talking as if this crazy scheme was a done deal!

"This simply isn't possible. I have my grandfather to consider," Jen reminded her boss.

"Where does he come into it?" Eli asked.

"I live with him…we have a chicken farm," she said grudgingly. "Granddad has severe arthritis, and he needs my help in the mornings. I don't start here until eleven."

"But I have a breakfast with my fan club at nine," he said.

Jen arranged her expression into one of mock sympathy. "I guess that's the end of that idea."

Eli laughed, evidently still finding her hilarious. "No problem. I'll have Kyle, one of our mechanics, come help your granddad. He's not needed at the track until after lunch and he grew up on a farm. I'm sure he can feed a few chickens."

"That'll work," Bob said. "Carlton, Jen's grandfather, is a big NASCAR fan. I'll bet he'd love the chance to talk racing with Kyle." He steepled his fingers. "Jen, Eli's had a difficult time the past few weeks. I'd like to help out if we can. I know it's not in your job description, but I'd be grateful."

Bob was a sucker for other people's problems. She could hardly object, since that was how she'd ended up here, despite having no knowledge of or enthusiasm for motorsports. Bob had willingly accommodated her personal situation—not only couldn't she afford to lose this job, she didn't want to let him down.

It's one lousy day. Bob needs my help. "Okay," she muttered. "I'll do it."

Eli's eyes were an emerald blaze of triumph.

She should have guessed a man like him wouldn't stop until he won.

ALTHOUGH THE RACE WASN'T until evening and the track didn't open to most fans until lunchtime, there were enough invitation-only events going on to make the track feel busy much earlier.

Jen took longer than expected to show Kyle the farm and introduce him to her grandfather—she'd told Granddad she needed to be at work early to help with driver liaison. So it was right at nine o'clock when she joined the line outside the tent on the infield where the Eli Ward Fan Club breakfast was being held.

Overnight, she'd convinced herself she was worrying about nothing. This was a working arrangement, so the fact she found Eli overpoweringly attractive was irrelevant. She would treat him like…like one of her granddad's chickens. She stifled a nervous giggle at the thought of clipping his wings.

"Sorry, miss, I don't have your name." The security guard on the door flipped the pages on his clipboard.

Jennifer felt her face warm as people muttered behind her. "I'm, uh, Eli's friend. He invited me yesterday."

"No name on the list, no entry."

If she needed further proof that Eli's invitation had been all about himself, not her, this was it. The line pressed forward, eager for her to move aside. She lowered her voice. "I'm his *girl*friend."

The guard snorted. See, she knew this was a dumb idea. Jen's shirt started sticking to her back.

"Is there a problem?" a male voice inquired behind her.

Jen turned to see two very tall, good-looking men. They weren't in the same league as Eli, but both exuded authority.

"Morning, Mr. Sizemore." The security guard stepped aside.

"Excuse me," Jen said, "is one of you Gil Sizemore?"

The taller of the two, who had slightly darker hair, said, "That's me."

Jen ignored the security guard's chuff of annoyance. "I wonder if I could come in with you? I'm Eli's date. Jen Ashby," she added belatedly.

Both men donned identical poker faces, only marginally less insulting than the guard's snort.

"You're with Eli?" Gil asked.

"Since when?" the other guy chipped in.

She and Eli had had about two minutes to agree on a story yesterday before his practice. She hoped she remembered it right.

"Eli spent some time in this area as a teenager." She was several years younger than her supposed boyfriend, so she was unlikely to have known him back then. She hoped the men would overlook that logic flaw. "I work for Bob Coffman. Eli and I ran into each other yesterday and he asked me to spend today with him."

She appreciated that Eli had come up with a script where every word was true. Even if the implication was misleading.

"So, you're not one of Eli's fans?" Gil asked.

"No, sir," she said fervently.

"Eli did mention he'd invited a guest to the breakfast," Gil admitted.

The other guy laughed. "Seems like he followed your advice, Gil." Before Jen could wonder what he meant, he stuck out a hand. "I'm Quinn Parrish from Rev Energy Drinks, Eli's sponsor." He flicked the brim of her track ball cap. "We'd better get you a Rev hat."

"The lady is with us," Gil told the guard as he ushered her into the tent. He glanced down at Jen. "Call me Gil."

She could tell just by looking at Gil he was smart. Perceptive. And she wasn't much of an actress. What chance did Eli's ruse have of success?

I just need to survive to the end of the race without making a fool of myself or letting Bob down. After the green flag fell, no one would be interested in chitchat. And when Eli crossed the finish line, her job would be done.

Inside the tent it was already sweltering. Predictably, Eli was in the middle of a knot of women in the center. He immediately broke out of the circle and headed for Jen.

In bed last night, she'd wondered if she'd exaggerated the impact of his masculine presence. Now, every cell in her body surfed a wave of longing.

"Jen, hi, I was worried you weren't going to make it." Eli's glance flicked over her rust-colored polo shirt and best jeans, his expression inscrutable. "I figured you for an early bird."

Another sparrow reference? No doubt he'd rather she was wearing something sexy, like half the women here, but her closet didn't contain anything that bared her midriff or clung to her very average curves.

"That would make you the worm," she pointed out.

Gil made a sound that might have been a cough.

Eli's eyes gleamed. "I see you've met Gil and Quinn." He took her hand, and held it loosely—but tight enough for a tingle to race up Jen's arm.

Gil watched the two of them. "You haven't forgotten what I said about distractions, Eli?"

"No, sir. Jen is quite the toughie. She'll keep me in line."

Gil's look measured her scant five feet four inches and turned quizzical. "In that case, welcome aboard, Jen."

When he and Quinn left to greet the fan club president, Eli said, "Smart move, acting like you don't adore me. Gil liked it."

"I *don't* adore you," she reminded him.

"Oh, yeah?" He raised their joined hands. "Then how do you explain this?"

"It's part of our act," she began, outraged...then realized he was teasing her again. "You're an idiot," she said. She couldn't help noticing he had capable hands, the fingers blunt and strong. Even though she did plenty of hard work on the farm, her hand looked soft in his.

"Actually I think I'm pretty smart." Eli glanced around. Several female fans hovered nearby, but hadn't approached. "This plan is working already."

The same scenario played out many times over the course of the day. With Jen beside him, fans respected Eli's personal space.

It was lucky she was under no illusion about his interest in her, because a girl could have her head turned by the teasing, charming consideration he bestowed. Not to mention the hand-holding, the arm around her shoulders, the occasional caress of a finger down her cheek.

Every contact sizzled so hot, the man should carry an inflammability warning label.

Eli seemed to have a hundred things to do, from bantering with his team to chatting with sponsors to discussing race strategy with Kevin Horton, and he seemed to want to do them all at once. The pace was dizzying. Frenetic. Yet Jen had to give him credit for taking the time to introduce her to people, to explain what was going on.

She couldn't believe he planned to race five hundred miles at full speed after a day like this. She was exhausted, but Eli seemed to gain energy with every new encounter.

As the 7:30 p.m. start of the race approached, he changed into his green-and-white uniform. It made his eyes more brilliant and accentuated his broad-shouldered, lean-hipped physique. When he appeared in the pits, Jen couldn't help a little intake of breath.

Eli smirked. "Let me guess, you're thinking *Mr. Irresistible.*"

She rolled her eyes. "It would be a striking combination on anyone." Then she betrayed the lie by adding, "Which came first—the uniform or the contact lenses?"

He laughed. "That'd be telling, chickadee."

Jen stepped over the pit wall to stand with Eli next to the No. 502 car. The seven team members permitted over the wall to service the car during his pit stops lined up behind them. All along pit road the tableau was repeated— crews fidgeted, drivers talked quietly with their wives or girlfriends. Most of those women were a lot taller and a lot prettier than Jennifer—she'd heard some of them were models. Supermodels, even. She wondered that no one had accused her of being an imposter. Guys like Eli didn't date girls like her.

After the invocation, a band struck up. The stirring words of the national anthem came over the sound system, sung by a young opera star. To Jen's bemusement, tears dampened her eyes as she joined in the singing.

Eli sang beside her, his voice deep, the notes true. He spotted the emotion in her face and raised his eyebrows, smiling as he sang.

Then it was time for the drivers to climb into their cars.

"Drive safely, Eli," Jen said.

"Thanks, chickadee." He leaned in, so close she could see the crinkle lines around his eyes from that smile he always wore. Then closer still.

She backed up. "What are you doing?"

His eyes were wide and innocent, green as spring grass, his drawl smooth as molasses. "Why, chickadee, I'm going to kiss you."

CHAPTER FIVE

Jen didn't miss the way Eli's smile turned devilish. All her danger sensors went on red alert. "No way do you get to kiss me."

"Look around," he invited, "and you'll see that going over the wall with a NASCAR driver is like making out at the movies."

She didn't believe that for one second. Until a glance to either side confirmed that women were puckering up all along pit road. The driver of the red-and-white car next to Eli's was locked in a passionate embrace with his wife.

"It's a NASCAR tradition," Eli said. "I can't race without the kiss."

"It's not part of our deal," she argued.

"The deal was, you would pose as my girlfriend. Girlfriends kiss their boyfriends." He eyed her mouth. "I'll keep it brief, Scout's honor."

"You were never a Boy Scout," she said with complete certainty.

He grinned. "Only because I moved around too much."

"You were expelled, more like it," she muttered. "For conning the Girl Scouts into kissing you."

Now he was laughing again. "Are we good for this, chickadee?"

Any more protest and she risked revealing just how much Eli disturbed her. He probably knew that already, but she didn't have to lose all dignity.

"Fine," she said stoically. "Go ahead."

Which made him laugh harder.

Then his hands went to her waist, anchoring her. "Ready, chickadee?"

No. Her breath came in short bursts. "Would you stop calling me that ridiculous—"

His lips met hers.

The kiss was as circumspect as she could want. But beneath the firmness of Eli's lips was a softness that teased. Taunted. Tantalized.

Jen's lips molded to his. Around them, the air hummed, a force-field of attraction. Eli's thumbs caressed the sides of her waist, and she made a little noise against his mouth. He captured the sound, echoed it, adjusted the angle of their bodies so that somehow they were closer together.

When he pulled away, Jen had to pour every ounce of effort into not letting her knees sag.

Eli ran a hand through his hair, his eyes still on her mouth. "Thanks, Jen."

He sounded dazed, as if that kiss had floored him.

If she let herself believe that, next thing she'd be putting out milk and cookies for Santa. The truth, she told herself ruthlessly, was that Eli had kissed dozens, hundreds of women. This couldn't have been special.

Whereas for her...

Somewhere deep inside her, there'd been a seismic shift.

Exactly what she'd feared, *known,* would happen with a man like him. He would forget the kiss by the time he started his engine. She would be haunted by it.

Eli touched her cheek. "Enjoy the race, chickadee." His tone was light as he turned to accept his helmet from one of the team, confirming that whatever she'd imagined about the kiss having an impact on him, she'd been wrong.

This whole day has been wrong.

"I quit," she blurted.

He paused, helmet in hand. "What?"

She made sure the team couldn't overhear before she continued. "I can't be your girlfriend anymore." The urge to make that clear was overpowering. She just wasn't sure if it was he who needed to know, or if she was warning herself. "I should get back to work where I belong."

His whole body went taut. "You agreed to watch the race here in the pits. Gil told me he's looking forward to introducing you to your first NASCAR race."

Gil had said that? Jen dismissed the small shock of pleasure. "You can't back out now," Eli continued. "Bob wants you to help me. That means seeing this thing through to the checkered flag."

Oh, yeah, play the Bob card. She shook her head to clear her muddled thoughts. "Fine, I'll watch the race," she said. "But that's all. No more girlfriend stuff. You can't…afterward…don't touch me again."

MORE THAN FOUR HUNDRED laps into the race, Eli was still riled by Jen's bizarre reaction to that kiss. Okay, so there'd been a sizzle that wasn't appropriate to a pretend relationship…big deal! He hadn't intended it, nor had she. It was just one of those man-woman chemistry things that sprang up fast and was as easily forgotten.

At least, he would have forgotten it by now if Jen hadn't acted so weird. Quitting on him!

"Trouble ahead, stay low," his spotter said into his earpiece.

Eli saw the tangle of cars up against the wall. He dived, just managing to dodge Ben Edmonds, running a lap behind. Edmonds was embroiled in a nightmare season; he hadn't had a win in years. He'd been married to his wife forever—Eli wondered if Gil had noticed that Edmonds wasn't exactly proof that a stable relationship was good for a guy's racing. Eli couldn't imagine being with the same woman day after day after day. No wonder rumor had it that the Edmonds' rock-solid marriage was crumbling under the pressure.

He thought again about Jen, about that chaste kiss that had packed so much punch. *Novelty value,* he told himself. If he did it again, it would bore him to tears.

So it didn't matter that she'd quit her girlfriend act early. Sure, she was pretty, but she wasn't the sort of woman who normally caught his attention. He would have no trouble refraining from kissing her after the race.

"Will Branch ahead," the spotter said. Almost without thinking, Eli zipped past on the high-banked Turn Two.

"Nice," Kevin, his crew chief, said over the headphones.

The word reminded Eli of Jen. She was a *nice* girl. Another good reason not to date her. *Nice girls are too much hard work.* Hadn't he spent most of the day entertaining her, aware that for her simply being in his presence didn't constitute a great time? He'd enjoyed himself, surprisingly so, but now, just thinking about how much hard work she'd been made him tired.

Or it would, once he got done with this race. This particular minute, adrenaline was pumping through him, leaving him supercharged.

Ahead of him, a white flag waved. Hell, he was on the last lap, and he had no idea what position he was. Eli hauled his focus into line and thumped the gas pedal to the floor for the last half-mile. In the closing seconds, he stole a pass on Rafael O'Bryan. His teammate wouldn't appreciate it, but Eli needed every point he could get.

"Sixth!" Kevin yelled as Eli swept past the checkered flag right behind Kent Grosso. "Great drive, man."

Eli felt no resentment toward the five drivers who'd beaten him. Hell, no. After the past few weeks, sixth place was a miracle.

He loosened his grip on the steering wheel a fraction as he headed all the way around the track to his frontstretch pit stall. As he puttered down pit road, he saw the Rev Energy Drinks sign waving; he pulled in.

Eli dropped his safety net and climbed out through the window opening.

Kevin grabbed him for a man-hug. "Congratulations, you were on fire out there."

"Thanks." Eli accepted the handshakes and pats on the back of his over-the-wall team, and thanked them individually for their contribution to today's result. His legs, still shaky after the grueling drive, were rapidly regaining their steadiness. He climbed over the wall, heading for Quinn and Gil—big smiles on both their faces—and Jen.

With her face alight with excitement, her eyes bright, her cheeks pink, she looked prettier than he remembered. It seemed as natural as breathing to kiss her. Then Eli remembered. Out of bounds. *My* ex-*girlfriend*.

He halted in his tracks, shocked at how cheated he felt.

"*That* was more like it," Gil said with satisfaction as he pumped Eli's hand.

"You had true star quality out there," Quinn added. Eli couldn't remember the guy ever saying anything so effusive. He tried to savor the moment, but a metallic taste in his mouth distracted him.

"Enjoy your first NASCAR race?" he asked Jen.

"Incredible." The word was a breath, a whisper that riffed across his senses.

"Enjoy?" Quinn's hoot was teasing, but friendly. "She went nuts, yelled her head off."

"Her enthusiasm made the race more fun for all of us," Gil said indulgently.

"I admit, it was spectacular." Jen's cheeks turned pinker and she said with reluctant honesty, "*You* were spectacular."

Damn, Eli wondered if he could have got away with kissing her after all. Then she dropped her gaze and he reminded himself it didn't matter. Their arrangement had always been temporary. There would be other girls. Women he could kiss without it being a big damn deal.

He turned his back on her. "I owe Kevin and the guys a drink," he told Gil. "They did a great job with that car."

Gil chuckled. "I don't let you blame the team when something goes wrong, so you're allowed to take the credit when it all pans out."

Eli wanted to ask, *Does this mean you won't fire me?*

"There's one other person who deserves some kudos," Gil said. "Seems young Jennifer played a big part in keeping you calm."

"I was listening in on your frequency. I've never heard you so quiet during a race," Quinn agreed.

Eli was a favorite of the fans who hired headsets to listen to the driver-crew chief communications because he talked more—a lot more—during the race than many other drivers. Kevin and Gil often suggested that if he shut up he might drive faster.

Had he been quieter today? Yeah. But not because Jen had magical calming properties. Because he'd been brooding about her unreasonable reaction to that kiss.

"I hope we'll see you in Atlanta," Gil said to Jen.

"Um…" She cast a beseeching look at Eli.

Hell, why hadn't he foreseen this complication? It should

have occurred to him his fake girlfriend and his boss would get along like a house on fire—he'd even accused her of being related to Gil!

"Jen won't—can't make Atlanta." He stumbled over the words.

Gil frowned. "Richmond, then. I suggest you hold on to this one, Eli. She's a keeper."

His tone was light, but the message wasn't. Gil liked Jennifer. Despite today's result, making the Chase for the NASCAR Sprint Cup was still a long shot. Would having Jen as his girlfriend help Eli keep his ride, even if he didn't make the Chase?

She quit, remember?

Jen fiddled with the lanyard that held her track pass. "Eli, I need to leave."

One more minute and she would walk away.

He had to make her stay.

A reporter approached, wanting to talk about the race.

"Don't go," Eli told Jen. "We need to talk."

He was certain he could convince her. She'd enjoyed his company as much as he'd enjoyed hers—yeah, okay, he might as well admit it.

As he answered the journalist's questions, he was aware of her shaking hands with Quinn, accepting Gil's kiss on the cheek. He willed her to wait.

At last the interview ended.

Eli turned back to Jen.

She was gone.

CHAPTER SIX

FREE RANGE CHICKENS might be happier and ultimately tastier than their cage-reared cousins, but raising them involved stepping in a lot of poop.

Jen sighed as she scraped the sole of one rubber boot against the bottom rung of the gate, dislodging the muck. This morning, everything was getting on her nerves.

After yesterday's race, life felt flat.

The farm, usually a haven of tranquility, seemed silent as a convent. And about as exciting.

Was it possible to miss the roar of forty-three engines? The smell of oil and rubber and gasoline? Or was it just a certain green-eyed driver with a lazy drawl whose absence she felt so keenly?

Jen realized she was touching her lips, and whipped her hand away.

I'm tired, is all. It wasn't yet seven-thirty and she'd stumbled out into the crisp morning air without benefit of coffee.

"Shoo, go on." She flapped her arms at a couple of hens taking their time about heading into the grassy area where they would spend most of the day. One of the birds flapped back, then skittered sideways in the right direction.

When they were all pecking excitedly at the grass as if they hadn't just pecked at the very same blades yesterday, she closed the gate.

And felt an alarming sense of kinship with those chickens.

Sure, they were certified free range. They could run around outside to their hearts' content. So long as they didn't want to go beyond the fence.

Tonight, they would be ushered back into the coop, and shut up until morning. And when they reached a respectable weight...

Jen didn't like to think about their fate.

Besides, any comparison with her own life stopped far short of the dinner table. So what if she occasionally felt trapped within the confines of her existence?

"I didn't feel like that before yesterday," she said out loud. The chickens ignored her. "And I don't feel like that now," she added, sounding defiant to her own ears.

No response from the birds. They obviously didn't know a lie when they heard it.

Truth was, Jen had been feeling out of sorts for a while. As if something was missing from her life. *I need to get back into my college studies.*

"I have plans," she told the chickens grandly. "I won't always be mucking out your coop."

One of the hens made a sound suspiciously like a cackle.

"You won't be laughing in a few weeks' time," she warned. She clapped a hand to her mouth. "I'm sorry, that was just plain mean."

"Nice to see you're as blunt with those birds as you are with me," said a voice behind her.

Eli!

Jen spun around. And absorbed the full impact of the NASCAR-driver-at-play package. A plaid shirt open over a faded navy blue T-shirt, worn jeans that hugged his hips.

Work boots that had somehow avoided any trace of poultry droppings.

She put a hand to her thudding heart. "What are you doing, sneaking up on me?"

He snickered. "If you hadn't been chatting with the chickens, you might have heard me coming."

"I wasn't chatting…" She gave up the argument in the face of overwhelming evidence. "Weren't you flying back to Charlotte last night?"

"I told the guys to go without me. I'll take a commercial flight this morning." He held the gate open for her with a flourish, as if he was ushering her into an opera house. Or some other place she'd likely never go.

Jen was horribly conscious of her unbrushed hair, and skin that hadn't seen moisturizer yet. Not to mention her ratty sweatshirt and frayed cutoffs….

"How did you get here?" she asked, hoping to distract Eli from the visual inspection he was now making.

"Rental car." His gaze reached her pink rubber boots; one eyebrow quirked. "I parked out front. Didn't see any sign of life, so thought I'd take a walk before I started waking people up."

"Granddad's awake, but his arthritis means he takes a while to get going," she said. "I do the early chores, starting with turning the chickens out into the yard."

Eli followed her toward the barn. "What happens now, chickadee?" He stopped, struck by a thought. "To think, I had no idea how appropriate that nickname is."

She glowered at him. "What happens now is I escort you to your car and point you toward the airport." She wasn't about to tell him it was time to muck out the shed. That would really set the seal on her glamorous existence.

Ignoring her hint, he set himself on course toward the house. As she finger-combed her hair, she tried to view the place through his eyes—a small, single-story dwelling sitting squat in the middle of a flat lawn, with a sag in the back porch to match the fences.

"Stop!" she ordered.

To her surprise, he obeyed. "What's up?"

She could hardly admit that if he took his gorgeous self one step closer to her everyday life, the contrast might make her explode from dissatisfaction.

She knotted her fingers. "Why are you here?"

He hooked his thumbs in the pockets of his jeans, managing to look relaxed and powerful in the same moment. "I want you back."

Jen's brain scrambled, much like the eggs she planned to eat for breakfast. "You want…what?"

"You dumped me," he said, "and now I want you back. I have to admit, chickadee—" one corner of his mouth kicked up "—this is unfamiliar territory for me."

Jen reined in her unruly thoughts, already charging down the road of he-really-likes-me. "But our arrangement was just for the race at Bristol. Why would you want…what you said?" It sounded too absurd to repeat.

He ran a hand over his chin; he hadn't shaved this morning and he looked…rugged. Real. Nothing like an unreliable, sex-symbol, out-of-her-reach race car driver.

She hoisted herself up onto the wooden fence, needing to take the weight off her suddenly weakened legs.

"I don't want to show up at my next race and have to confess to Gil that we broke up," he said. "You did such a great job yesterday, he'll be on my case for letting you go."

She tugged her cutoffs down where they'd ridden high up her thighs.

Eli's glance flicked over her. "You have great legs."

To her irritation, he sounded surprised.

"You think admiring my legs will make me fall into your arms?" she demanded.

He rubbed his chin again, and she imagined the sensuous roughness of stubble. "Chickadee, you seem somewhat preoccupied with my ability to make women fall at my feet, into my arms, wherever. The simple fact is, I didn't get to see your legs yesterday, and now I'm noticing they are very nice." He spread his hands as if to say, is that a crime?

"Stay on topic," she said. "Surely yesterday's race proved to Gil that you can focus on your driving."

"You'd think." He shoved his hands in his pockets. "Unfortunately it wasn't enough. If I don't make the Chase—you know what that is, right?"

She nodded. "Quinn told me."

"Did he also tell you Rev Energy Drinks will pull its sponsor dollars and Gil's threatened to fire me?"

"I—no! That's awful."

"I plan to make the Chase," Eli assured her. "But it won't be easy and it's not all up to me."

"Gil didn't seem unreasonable," Jen said, uncertain.

"He's not. Mostly. But if he's seriously ticked off, he might fire me anyway, even if another driver takes me out, no fault of mine." Eli put his hands either side of her on the fence rail. His mouth was almost level with hers.

She diverted her gaze over his shoulder.

"Gil's less likely to sack me if he thinks I'm doing things his way," Eli said. "If you and I keep up our act through to at least Richmond…"

Jen snapped her eyes back to him. "That's weeks away!"

He nodded. His expression was neutral, but she discerned tension in his grip on the fence. One thing she'd learned yesterday was that NASCAR drivers faced intense pressure. A wave of sympathy washed over her.

"Surely Gil knows," she suggested, "those lightning-quick reactions you have on the track are the flipside of your distractibility." She'd been amazed how Eli could seize an opportunity almost before his rivals knew it existed.

"I guess." He scratched the back of his neck, frowning.

"And the way you kept changing strategy on the fly, all through the race. That's part of the same quality."

"For someone who never watched a NASCAR race before, you picked up a lot," he said.

"I guess I picked up enough to respect what you do," she admitted.

His eyes widened in feigned shock. "You mean, you accept that driving a stock car is a real job?"

She waggled her hand to signify *maybe,* since he didn't need any more adulation in his life. "I'm not saying it's in the same league as plumber, or cop…"

"Or chicken farmer?" he suggested.

"Hmm," she said thoughtfully as she pretended to assess him. Her scrutiny swiftly deteriorated into outright ogling of the planes of his face, his broad shoulders, the muscled physique that made him the perfect poster boy for Rev Energy Drinks. Jen drew a pleasurable breath, aware that something—the morning sun?—was going dangerously to her head. "I'm not sure you'd make it as a chicken farmer."

That piece of nonsense somehow warmed Eli's gaze. "Cruel," he murmured. Then, before she could figure what he was up to, his hands went to her waist and he swung her off the fence in one smooth movement.

"Put me down!" she squawked.

He planted her in front of him, still holding her. "I like you, Jen," he said. "You're good company. I get that you don't want to date a guy like me for real…"

Darn it, she couldn't stop staring at his lips. The only

consolation was he seemed to have a similar fixation with hers.

"But I'd sure appreciate it," he said huskily, "if you'd come back to me."

He liked her. Eli Ward had said he liked her! What if, although they'd started off pretending at romance, he really did think that kiss was special, after all? What if, beneath the NASCAR glitz, he was just an ordinary guy—no, he could never be ordinary. But what if he was a guy with a problem, just like everyone had problems? And she could help?

"What about my job, and Granddad?" she prevaricated, aware her motives weren't entirely altruistic. The tedium of this morning's routine had made one thing startlingly clear; she *wanted* to spend time with Eli.

"I'll pay someone to help your grandfather when you're not here. I can talk to Bob about your work." He released her waist, and she missed his touch immediately. "Anyone else I need to convince?" he asked. "Your parents?"

She shook her head. "My parents are dead."

"Jen, I'm sorry." He touched a knuckle to her cheek, and she wanted to lean into his hand.

"It was a long time ago. I was only a year old, I don't even remember them." Which was just one of the many things she hadn't forgiven her parents for.

"So your grandfather raised you?"

"He and Nan," she agreed. "Since Nan died, it's been just me and Granddad."

"And the chickens," Eli reminded her.

She smiled. "And the chickens."

He kicked at a fence post. "Do you mind if I ask what happened to your folks?"

She appreciated his interest. "My dad was an ornithologist—rare birds. He was on a two-year expedition, me and my mom in tow, to find a bird everyone else thought was extinct. We were caught up in flooding in Indonesia."

"You were there when your parents died?" he asked, shocked.

"I was too young to know anything about it. But, yeah, I was one of those miracle survival stories. My parents left me with the wife of their native guide, along with all our passports and papers. My reunion with Nan and Granddad made headlines around the world." More than enough fame for her. She bit her lip.

"I'm sorry," he said again.

"Me, too." She couldn't help the grimness in her voice. "If my parents hadn't been so caught up in the legend of that bird…"

Eli touched her hand. "Accidents happen."

"When people do stupid things," she finished automatically. Her grandparents had drummed that into her over the years.

He frowned. "I was going to say, accidents happen to anyone, anytime." The sweep of his arm encompassed the barn and the yard. "You could slip over on some chicken sh-stuff and break your neck."

"Unlikely," she scoffed. "If my parents had stayed at home and taken regular jobs, they wouldn't have drowned." Another point the passage of time hadn't blunted, as far as her grandfather was concerned.

"Some people," Eli said carefully, "feel that kind of life would stifle them. Like they'd die of boredom if—" He winced. "Damn, I didn't mean…"

Too late.

Jen felt a rush of moisture behind her eyes. "It's not *boring* to face up to your responsibilities." She stomped away from him, then wheeled around. "It's not *boring* to earn an honest living." Her chest constricted as guilt and anger warred. Because even as she rejected his irresponsible attitude, a part of her agreed with him. Then she found an ultimate truth to cling to: "It's not boring to be there for your kid, for someone you love."

Eli raked a hand through his hair. "I'm sorry it didn't happen that way for you, Jen. But you can't go blaming your parents for living a life that made them happy. If they'd lived, you probably would have grown up with the same sense of adventure. You'd be wandering the world right now."

His words were an assault on everything she valued: home, family, loyalty.

"There's more to life than traveling the world with a buck and a backpack, or driving a race car in the hope of finding fame and fortune," she snapped. "But I wouldn't expect you to see that. Go find yourself another girlfriend, Eli. Someone less *boring*."

CHAPTER SEVEN

ELI CROSSED THE SUN-FADED grass, then walked around the side of Jen's house to the rutted driveway where he'd left his car. Not that he was about to "go find another girlfriend." He had the fake girlfriend he wanted right here, and he wouldn't leave until she said yes.

A few minutes ago, he'd thought they were in perfect accord—sexual attraction sparking like crazy, kidding around, a healthy dose of mutual liking and respect…hell, most of his real relationships hadn't had as much going for them.

Then she'd turned all weird again. He wished to hell she'd be more predictable, like the other women he dated.

He sighed in frustration. Normally, in the rare event a woman didn't want to go out with him, he would cut and run. But Gil liked Jen. For once in his life, Eli couldn't just move on.

He made a sharp right turn and climbed the steps to the front porch.

"Where are you going?" Jen chased after him.

The frosted glass front door was unlocked. It squeaked as it opened. Eli walked into a narrow hallway lined with family photographs. Looking for something, anything he could use to convince her that, given how well they got along and the spark between them, faking a relationship for a few weeks should be no hardship. His life as a NASCAR

Sprint Cup Series driver was at stake. The one thing he couldn't give up without a fight.

Jen bustled in behind him. "I insist you leave."

He stopped, and she bumped into him. Automatically he steadied her, his fingers wrapped around her slim, strong arms. Their gazes locked, and Eli's veins zinged. Like they did when he was in a race car and the green flag was about to fall. *Seize the Day.*

"Jen? Is someone there?" The voice came from down the hall.

Eli let go of Jen and followed it.

In the modest living room, her grandfather sat in a recliner—one of the original models back from when those things were invented, Eli judged—in front of the TV set. Which was switched off. When he saw Eli the old man's brows drew together, much the same way his granddaughter's frequently did. "Who are you?" he barked.

"Granddad, this is Eli Ward." Jen's eyes flashed daggers at Eli as she made the introduction.

"Don't get up, sir," Eli said, as the old man began a laborious struggle to his feet.

Like his granddaughter, he did things his own way. He huffed and puffed until he was upright, then his left hand gripped the back of the chair while he reached his right to Eli.

"Carlton Ashby," he introduced himself.

Eli shook his hand.

The older man looked him over. "I wondered if the TV made your hair look longer, but I see it needs a cut in real life."

Eli nodded. NASCAR fans either loved the length of his hair or hated it—it wasn't something he was prepared to debate.

"Not a bad drive yesterday," Carlton commented.

"Thank you." Eli figured it was high praise.

"You have a good day at work?" Carlton asked Jen. It dawned on Eli the old guy hadn't seen her since she arrived home late after the race.

"Fine, thanks, Granddad."

"Did you meet Kent Grosso?" Carlton asked.

She shook her head. "I don't think so."

So, he was a Grosso fan. Kent, with his multigeneration family ties to NASCAR and a wife to whom he was devoted, was arguably the closest driver in NASCAR to an ordinary guy in a regular job. If you forgot he was a celebrity.

"Dennis Crane stopped by yesterday," Carlton said. "His grandson, the boy that likes you, will be home for Thanksgiving."

The hairs at the back of Eli's neck stood to attention.

"That's nice," Jen said without enthusiasm.

"He's a steady young man," her grandfather pointed out.

Who Jen dates is none of my business. Eli rubbed his neck and forced himself to relax as he gazed around the Ashbys' living room, which was as ordinary as any he'd seen. Except for that stack of accounting textbooks on the dining table.

"Those are Jen's." Carlton caught him looking. "She's studying business at the community college." He added proudly, "Gets straight As, too."

Jennifer made a shushing motion. "Eli doesn't want to hear about my *boring* degree."

I really screwed up, dammit.

"What do you plan to do after you graduate?" Eli had to admit, an accounting degree did sound boring.

"No idea," she said shortly. "That's a long way away."

"She's taking next semester off, working extra hours

at the track," Carlton said. "But after that, she'll be back into it."

Money, Eli thought. Jen was probably slowing her studies so she could earn enough to support herself and her grand-dad. He examined his surroundings. This house hadn't seen any attention in years. Doubtless Carlton's arthritis chewed up a fortune in medical bills. The chicken farm was a minuscule operation, as far as he could see.

Eli had lacked family, lacked permanence in his life, but he'd never lacked money.

Money was convenient; it got things done.

Things like, making sure he had his Gil-approved "girl-friend" in Atlanta.

"Okay, I'll go now," he told Jen abruptly.

"But why are you here?" Carlton asked, suddenly realizing how odd it was to have Eli in his house.

"Jen thought you might like to meet me, being a NASCAR fan and all."

Carlton's brow furrowed. "But I like Kent Grosso."

Eli couldn't help smiling. "I see where Jen gets her bluntness. Thanks for letting me visit, sir." He shook Carlton's hand with an enthusiasm that wasn't entirely returned.

"I'll see you out," Jennifer said, as he knew she would. She would want to be sure he left.

Out in the hallway, she brushed past him to open the front door. Eli was shocked at how that glancing touch made him want to try that kiss all over again.

"Goodbye, Eli." She held the door wide open.

"Ten thousand dollars," he said.

She stared.

Eli took the door from her unresisting fingers and closed it. "That's how much I'll pay you to spend the next three weekends posing as my girlfriend."

"Are you insane?" Her cheeks turned scarlet. "Do you have any idea how much money that is?"

"Less than I make in a week," he said calmly. It was only a small fraction of his salary, but he figured that information would outrage rather than impress. "Enough for you to pay someone to help out around here while you speed up your degree. I'm also offering you a fifty percent share of any prize money I earn during those three weeks. Though I wouldn't count on that," he said fairly. "I haven't won much money this year."

"You need to leave." But her voice was unsteady.

"Those plans for your future that you were discussing with the chickens…" He ignored her deep flush. "Are you going to turn down an opportunity to make them reality, just because I offended you?"

JEN'S HANDS SHOOK. She wedged them into the pockets of her cutoffs. Ten thousand dollars!

All she had to do was pretend to be Eli's girlfriend, which she'd been on the verge of agreeing to anyway, until he reminded her of the great gulf between their attitudes.

As if that mattered in a fake relationship! Which was all this would be, she reminded herself. Despite that brief hope their kiss had meant something to him, if she analyzed his words, nothing he'd said suggested they would genuinely be dating. Real girlfriends didn't get paid!

Ten thousand dollars.

"It sounds like a bribe," she said.

"It's a job offer," he corrected. "A temporary job to help secure your future. Compared with what I stand to lose, ten thousand bucks is chicken feed. Literally, in this case."

Ten thousand dollars would bring the security she craved closer. But it would do more than that. The sooner she finished her degree, the sooner she could get a good-paying job and stop feeling as if she was missing out on life.

"Why didn't you mention the money earlier?" she asked. "Why pretend that you like me?" It seemed her every encounter with him was designed to batter her pride.

"I do like you," he said, without a trace of that teasing smile. "But that wasn't enough. Then I saw you need money…I like to seize the day."

The second time he'd quoted that axiom. Life was seldom as simple as such mottos suggested.

Could it be that simple now? Granddad would freak out at what he'd call a "harebrained scheme," Jen posing as Eli's girlfriend. *Granddad doesn't need to know.* She could "work" for Eli, and when it was all over, she could date Dennis Crane's grandson. Who was a nice enough guy…a plumber, actually.

Though she'd never felt much attraction toward him.

She thought about spending weekends with Eli. About kissing him. Which shouldn't be on her mind at all.

But it was. And now the money gave her the excuse to do what she was dying to do.

CHAPTER EIGHT

CARLTON ASHBY bought the story that Jen was taking a temporary job as Eli's assistant. With no race at Bristol next week and only a local meeting the following two weekends, Bob Coffman was more than happy to release Jen from some of her hours.

There was no NASCAR Sprint Cup Series race scheduled the following weekend, either, but Eli invited Jen to accompany him to a charity gala in Charlotte. Those semisocial events were worse than races when it came to persistent fans.

Eli grinned to himself as he put the finishing touches to the BLT sandwiches he was assembling for an early lunch.

He'd met Jen at the airport an hour ago, brought her to his house on Lake Norman, settled her and her small overnight bag into his largest guestroom. Now she was perched on a bar stool on the other side of the kitchen island.

Everything was going just right. Gil had been delighted to hear Jen would be in Charlotte, and then at the Atlanta race. He'd lightened up on his scrutiny, which had given Eli the chance to meet informally with a couple of other team owners this week to talk about his prospects.

Best of all—at least, it felt best of all with her sitting right here, wearing faded jeans and a white T-shirt that looked unintentionally sexy, as if they'd shrunk in the wash—their arrangement gave him a license to kiss her again.

"You want avocado salsa on this?" Eli asked Jen.

"Sure, thanks."

Okay, so things weren't a hundred percent just right. Jen had barely spoken since she arrived—where was that bluntness he enjoyed? If her nerves, or whatever it was, didn't pass soon, their act wouldn't be convincing.

"I'd better give you our agenda for the day," he said as he smeared the salsa on her sandwich. "Gil will be here in about half an hour, with a reporter from the *Observer*. She's writing an in-depth feature about Double S Racing."

Jen's brown eyes widened. "You don't need me for that, do you?"

"Believe it or not, the reporter has me pegged as the team's wild card. Gil wants her to see my 'more settled side.'"

She nibbled on her lower lip. "Won't it just confirm her suspicions when you and I break up after Richmond?"

"The article will be out by then." She definitely had the nicest-looking mouth Eli had seen in a long time, he thought, as that bottom lip caught again. "We should probably throw in a PDA or two," he said casually.

"PDA?"

"Public display of affection." He reached across the island, caressed the back of her hand with his thumb. "You sure have soft skin for a gal who works on a farm."

She didn't reply, but this time it was a good silence—she appeared mesmerized by the movement of his thumb. Eli was finding it pretty hypnotic himself.

What was wrong with him? Since when had touching a woman's hand been a major turn-on? He'd been on this "good, clean living" kick too long, he thought, disgusted. With one early night after another, it had been the longest week of his life.

He pushed a plate with a sandwich across to Jen, then

carried his own around the island. He sat on the stool next to hers.

"After the interview, Cara Stallworth will take you shopping for a dress for tonight," he said. "She's married to Jeb Stallworth, another driver. You'll like her."

"I brought a dress with me," Jen protested.

"This charity gala will be a black tie, red-carpet affair," he explained. "There'll be some pretty fancy duds. I want you to feel comfortable." He took a bite of his sandwich. "Don't worry, I'm paying—this is on top of the ten grand."

She frowned. Had she forgotten this was a business arrangement? *Uh-oh.* After a moment, she nodded, to his relief.

"Then you have a haircut with Rue Larrabee at the Cut 'N' Chat," he said briskly.

"If anyone needs a haircut, it's you," she said.

That was more like the Jen he knew. He grinned. "Are you kidding? My hair's practically a sex-symbol trademark."

She snorted, reassuring him further.

"Most of the women there tonight will have had their hair done specially," he said.

"Oh, all right," she grumbled. She squinted. "But don't even think about suggesting colored contact lenses."

He laughed, the tedium of the week falling away. "There's something I should tell you, chickadee. I don't wear contacts."

She set her sandwich down on her plate. Swallowed. "That's…your real eye color?"

He nodded. She leaned forward, peering into his eyes.

"I feel like such an idiot." She pressed her palms to her cheeks and it made her look cuter than ever.

"An easy mistake to make," he said graciously.

He might have guessed she'd take it more seriously.

"I could have asked Gil about your eyesight problems any time last weekend," she fretted. "What would he have thought?"

"Same as I do, that you're a little odd."

She swatted him. Eli grabbed hold of her hand, held it in place, a small, warm caress against his bare forearm.

"What else should I know about you?" she asked.

"Hmm, let me think."

She tensed as he dabbed a finger against a smidgeon of avocado at the corner of her mouth.

"I have all my own teeth and hair," he said.

She laughed, the sound fading as he transferred the avocado to his own mouth. If he wasn't mistaken, and he seldom was where women were concerned, there was hunger in Jen's eyes. The sooner they got to that kiss, the better.

"Eli," she said, tugging her fingers free, "this weekend is more complicated than watching a race. You said yourself this reporter has an agenda where you're concerned. I need to know more about you."

Eli lifted the top off his sandwich and shook salt over it. "Like what?"

"Tell me about your family. Do any of them live here with you?"

"It's just me." He remembered how small her grandfather's house was. This showy, glass and concrete palace made it look even tinier.

"Most of the drivers have places like this," he defended himself. "I don't own it, I have a one-year rental agreement." Another fact it would be useful for her to know before the interview. She was right, he should have briefed her better. "I might try Mountain Island Lake next. Chad and Zack Matheson live out there."

Her forehead creased. "Surely you can afford to buy a house?"

"What's the point when I'll likely want a change a year or so down the track?"

"Most people want a home of their own."

"Home," he said, "is overrated."

He could tell he'd shocked her, but she didn't say anything, just held her sandwich away from her mouth and inspected it as if she expected to find a bug. Fine by him; he didn't want to argue.

"So where do your parents live?" she asked.

He took a bite, chewed and swallowed. "They died when I was a kid. Car accident. I'm an orphan, like you."

"Eli, that's awful." She looked more upset than she had when she'd told him about her own parents.

He lifted one shoulder. "It happened…nothing I can do about it."

"So who did you live with after they died?"

He didn't want to dig that up now. "Who *didn't* I live with?" he quipped. "Mom and Dad left me well provided for financially, and I had plenty of relatives willing to do their bit. But it was hard for anyone to commit to a permanent addition to the family. I moved around."

She flushed. "That's why you had multiple ninth-grade English teachers. You weren't expelled."

"I'm not as reprehensible as you'd like to think," he agreed.

She tilted her head to one side, her eyes warm with concern. "Oh, Eli."

"Don't even think about getting on a 'poor Eli' kick," he warned. "I learned to make friends quickly, and walk away without a backward glance when I had to. I learned that whether you're in a good situation or not-so-good, there's always another opportunity ahead. Lessons that have served me well."

"I see." A piece of bacon had fallen onto her plate. She

popped it into her mouth, reminding Eli about that kiss again. Dammit, everything she did reminded him of the kiss.

"Did anyone teach you that loyalty, the ability to stick around when things get tough, is important?" she asked. "That anything worth having is worth fighting for?"

"I know all that," he said dismissively. Apart from racing in the NASCAR Sprint Cup Series, he couldn't think of anything much he'd fight for.

She wiped her lips with a paper napkin—the kiss again, dammit!—and said slowly, deliberately, "Did anyone teach you they would love you through thick and thin?"

He jolted back in his seat, her words a slap in the face.

"Stop it," he ordered.

"Stop what?"

"You've got that crusading look in your eye, like when you're lecturing me about contraception or my responsibility to my unborn children. I know everything I need to about… about relationships." He was damned if he was going to talk about *love* with her. It was the one word he assiduously avoided with his real dates and it was even more off the table with a fake girlfriend.

"I have friends in every county in a fifty-mile radius," he said. "The reason you're here, don't forget, is because I have too many people in my life."

"Fans who wouldn't look twice at you if you weren't a NASCAR driver."

Dammit, she had a nerve. Eli clattered their plates together, taking the opportunity to break eye contact as he cleared them away. "More than a few of those women think I'm charming in my own right."

"You're very charming," she agreed. "Tell me, Eli, what happens when you're not charming? Who's going to stick around when you *don't* have your own teeth and hair?"

He recoiled.

"Because that's what matters," she said.

"That's what matters to *you*." He regained his equilibrium, slanted her a flirty smile. "What matters to me is enjoying the moment. Which, frankly, chickadee, you're making difficult with all this girl-talk."

"You don't think knowing you're loved would make even the most ordinary moment more enjoyable?" she persisted. She had the nerve to look sorry for him, nibbling on the corner of one thumbnail.

Eli staged a yawn. "Shucks, chickadee, what would a guy like me know about ordinary moments?"

GIL AND THE REPORTER, Marion Galton, arrived five minutes ahead of schedule.

Jen sat next to Eli on the couch for the interview, his arm slung along the back of the cushion so that his fingertips rested on her shoulder, their caress as light as a summer breeze.

His touch distracted her from processing their earlier discussion—she wouldn't be surprised if that was the whole point. She'd learned that somewhere beneath the flirty, flighty Eli Ward, the real Eli Ward was carefully fenced-off. Because the real Eli Ward was vulnerable.

If he'd been attractive to her before, discovering he had hidden depths made him truly, ironically irresistible. Just like the magazine said.

Marion, the reporter, was firmly focused on the superficial. Her eyes raked Eli with a blatancy that would have been questionable had their genders been reversed.

"So, how did you two meet?" she asked.

Eli trotted out the story they'd agreed on. His index finger drew lazy circles on Jen's shoulder, but she sensed a latent pressure. He was annoyed by her breaching his defenses.

Too bad. Because the real Eli Ward took intriguing to a new level.

"Very romantic," the woman cooed when he finished. "Are you two serious?"

"We've only just reconnected," he said. "Ask me again in a couple of months." By then, of course, her article would have been printed.

"If you two are still dating in a couple of months, I won't need to ask," the woman joked. "That would be a record for you."

Eli's mouth tightened. "The length of my past relationships isn't relevant to this interview."

Jen couldn't agree more. Besides, it didn't take a rocket scientist to see that the lack of permanent relationships in his youth had made Eli commitment-shy. All those women, all those connections made on the basis that it wouldn't hurt when they were severed.

"What about the length of your professional relationships?" Marion asked.

Eli paused. "I'm not sure what your question is."

Marion leaned forward. "Is it true you're looking for a new ride? That you've been interviewing with other teams?"

CHAPTER NINE

THE SILENCE WAS ABSOLUTE…and rapidly turning grim.

Gil might have been made of granite, for all the expression he showed.

Eli's gut churned. He had to answer the question. Even if it was to refuse to answer. A giveaway in itself.

Then Jen took his hand. Laced her small fingers through his. Squeezed.

It was as if he'd been given permission to breathe.

Eli let out a little air. Sucked some more in. Not enough, but it helped.

"You spoke to Taney Motorsports, I believe?" Marion prompted. "And Fulcrum Racing?"

A hiss from Gil, which the reporter noticed. His boss would be furious with himself for betraying his anger. Eli should never have told Gil how much he admired Fulcrum.

"Marion, are you aware of Eli's personal motto?" Jen asked.

His head jerked around. She squeezed his fingers again.

"Seize the Day," she said. "Carpe diem."

That was it, the Latin words. Eli felt a sneaking sense of pride in his fake girlfriend, which didn't make a lot of sense.

"Your point is?" the woman asked.

"You might also know that last year Eli had more top-five finishes than any previous Cup rookie," Jen continued. Someone had been doing her homework. For a woman who cherished the dream of an ordinary life, she sure as hell was unpredictable.

"He also had a higher than average number of DNFs."

Jen waved away Eli's Did Not Finish record. "You don't get that close to the checkered flag that often unless you know how to seize the day. Strategy only goes so far."

Eli recognized one of Gil's favorite lines, and glanced at his boss. Gil's mouth was set in a forbidding line.

"Eli's impetuous," Jen said. "He goes with his gut. Mostly it pays off. Sometimes, though, he gets ahead of himself."

Where was she getting this stuff? Which coincidentally happened to be true. He thought about interrupting her, but anything she said had the advantage of not being official team comment. He or Gil could "correct" her later.

The reporter was scribbling notes to back up her recorder. Eli hoped that was a good thing.

"Fact is, Gil's a demanding owner who expects a lot of his drivers. He makes it clear they need to deliver results," Jen said. Oh, crap! She was all but admitting Gil had threatened to fire him!

Marion's face brightened. "So you're saying Eli's poor results this season—"

"I'm saying Eli's nature dictates he'll do whatever he needs to in order to drive in the NASCAR Sprint Cup Series."

Damn. They'd skated close enough to the edge. Eli took over. "Gil Sizemore gave me the break I needed to move into Cup racing," he said. "If I can meet his standards, I can meet anybody's. But I hope to keep meeting the Double S standard for a long time."

He'd put the blame for any future career change squarely in Gil's court.

"Eli and I are on the same page," Gil said.

Eli wondered if the woman realized that wasn't a promise not to fire him. Gil was saying he needed to improve his driving.

After some more roundabout discussion, the reporter left. When Eli returned to the living room from showing her out, Jen and Gil were engaged in a stand-off in front of the empty fireplace. Jen's hands were fisted on her hips.

Gil swung to face him. "Give me one good reason why I shouldn't fire you right now."

"Gil!" Jen darted forward, inserting herself between them. "I don't want to tell you how to run your business—"

"Then don't," Gil said, managing to sound both menacing and the complete gentleman.

Jen ignored him. "But I can tell you, when chickens feel unsafe, they stop laying, they stop gaining weight, they stop doing any of the things they should."

"Chickens?" Gil echoed, at the same time as Eli.

"You have got to stop threatening Eli," Jen chided him. "Some people react well to stress. Eli doesn't."

What the—? "I'm not a chicken," Eli protested.

"That's true," she said. "Every chicken I know is braver than you."

Which at least produced a spurt of laughter from Gil.

"I understand you're from a close family," Jen said to Gil. "You have no idea what a difference that makes to your confidence."

"Eli has plenty of confidence," Gil said, but he sounded less aggressive.

"He's confident he can take care of himself," Jen agreed. "You need him to be confident in the team so he can focus on winning, not on where he's going to be working tomorrow."

"Butt out, Jen," Eli warned. He could fight his own

battles. Gil wasn't dismissing her views—which probably meant he'd be sending Eli to a shrink next week.

"Someone has to stand up for you," she said.

"I'll echo Eli's sentiment, if not his word choice," Gil said coldly. "Eli's employment is between me and him. And right now, it's hanging by a thread."

Eli felt chilled to the bone. How dare Jen poke her nose into his life, make things worse by blabbing to that reporter about the tension between him and Gil?

She'd way overstepped the mark. The women he dated knew the score: keep it light, keep it brief, move on.

This fake relationship is so over. He was better off without her. They would get through tonight's gala, then he'd tell her the bad news. *You're dumped.*

"JEN?" ELI RAPPED on the guestroom door. "You ready?"

He'd thrown on his tuxedo in two minutes, and been waiting for Jen ever since. He glanced at his watch. What was taking so long?

"Coming." Her voice was muffled.

Eli scowled at the closed door. He hadn't seen her since Cara had turned up to take her shopping. Smart lady that she was, Cara had discerned the strain between him and his so-called girlfriend—she'd put a protective arm around Jen, who she didn't even know, and given Eli a look through narrowed eyes.

He couldn't exactly tell Cara that Jen had psychoanalyzed him in front of a reporter, scolded his boss and accused Eli of being a fraidy-cat.

He couldn't tell anyone how mad he was, he realized. As Jen said, the people around him were there for the good times.

Dammit. "Hurry up, Jen," he called. The later they arrived at this shindig, the more of an entrance they would make, and right now he had a strong preference for a low profile. He hoped Cara had found Jen a nice outfit. Preferably one that didn't involve a ball cap, cute though she looked in those things.

She's not cute, she's the demon girlfriend from hell.

The bedroom door opened.

A hundred words fired through Eli's mind and not one of them was *cute*.

Sexy, gorgeous, amazing…

"What's wrong?" In a pose that was purely provocative but also, he'd bet, a hundred percent unintentional, Jen rested one arm on the doorjamb.

The movement drew his attention to her curves in the peach-colored dress that clung in the kinds of places his mind wasn't meant to be exploring. "I…uh…" he said, his mouth dry.

"You don't like it?" she said nervously. Then realization dawned and a very feminine smile curved her mouth. "You *do* like it!"

"It's not bad," he groused.

Her face fell, and he felt like a heel. *She deserves it.* Then she stepped past him, and there was a wiggle in her hips that hadn't been there before. She glanced back over her shoulder. "Are you ready?" she asked, her voice cooler and more sophisticated than he liked to hear from her.

He nodded. Then cleared his throat. "I like your hair." Though he only said it to make up for hurting her feelings about the dress, there was no doubt her hair was pretty, curled loosely around her shoulders, highlights gleaming where the light caught them.

She grinned, delighted, the sophisticate act gone. She twirled a lock around her finger. "Just as well, since you spent a small fortune on it."

As he held the car door open for Jen, Eli rethought his

plans for the evening. Not about dumping her; he still planned to do that. But maybe he'd get that kiss in first.

JEN FELT LIKE CINDERELLA at the ball. She'd never seen such a glittering crowd. The gala was in aid of a charity supporting people who'd suffered life-altering injuries in road accidents. NASCAR drivers and team owners had turned out in force to lend their support. The result was wall-to-wall glamour.

The thing about Cinderella and the ball, Jen reminded herself, *is that when midnight comes, it's all over.* The way Eli had looked at her when she'd called him a chicken, she'd be lucky to last that long.

But someone had to defend him. Gil didn't get to play fast and loose with something as important to Eli as his career. That reporter didn't get to heap all the blame on Eli for the discord at Double S Racing.

She glanced at his profile as they shook hands along the reception line. She could tell he was also still mad that she'd called him on the lack of intimacy, of loyalty, in his life. No one else would guess at his hostility, not with his mouth curved in that affable smile, and him holding her hand with every evidence of relaxation. But she saw it in the tension of his facial muscles.

It was a shame he couldn't understand that she related far better to the glimpse she'd had of his loneliness than she did to his charming, disheveled Greek god persona. It made him…ordinary.

When they got past the receiving line, the first person they ran into was Gil, talking with a couple of other team owners. At least that meant he couldn't snub them without generating a ton of gossip.

Eli took the initiative. "Evening, Gil."

"Hello, Eli, Jen," Gil said, a bite to his tone.

To Jen's surprise, Eli tugged her closer.

"Hi, Gil," she said, with a nip of her own. And was surprised again, when Eli's lips twitched.

"You look delightful," Gil complimented her, with the distant Charleston charm he did so well.

"Thanks," Jen replied. "Eli is so wonderfully thoughtful that he arranged for Cara Stallworth to take me shopping for a dress."

Gil's eyebrows rose slightly. "Thoughtful indeed."

She couldn't tell if he was being sarcastic, so she squeezed Eli's fingers in case he needed reassurance.

They moved on, crossing the enormous room.

"I don't need you defending me to Gil," Eli muttered, close to her ear. "Or to anyone."

"You bring out my protective instincts," she said.

He gaped. "What?"

"You heard." She tried her own variation of his smirk, and was gratified to see it annoyed him. How could she ever have found him intimidating?

"Are you going to stop talking that crap," he demanded, "or do I have to walk away?"

They'd reached the table occupied by some of the clients of the charity they were there to help. People who'd suffered all kinds of injuries, many of them still visible, eager now to meet Eli. They didn't need him distracted by his anger with her.

"You don't need to walk away," she said. "I will."

She left him glaring after her and went to talk to Cara and her husband, Jeb, who was so crazy about his new wife, it was almost painful to watch.

Jen kept an eye on Eli, who'd sloughed off his annoyance with her to chat to the accident victims. Even from here, she could see he was entirely natural with them, unfazed by physical incapacity, scarring or even mental disability. She wondered if meeting these people made him think about his parents' fatal accident.

Bart Branch, one of the few NASCAR drivers she recognized, asked Jen to dance. He was pleasant company, so they danced through several songs. After Bart returned her to the Stallworths, she had no shortage of dance partners.

But the whole time she was aware of Eli. How could someone so shallow, so willing to walk out of a relationship or a job at the first sign of discomfort, see beyond the damaged surface into the hearts of the people he was still engrossed in conversation with?

Because that's what he wants someone to do for him.

Could that be true? Could this man who specialized in superficial relationships, want someone to look deeper, despite his protestations to the contrary? He'd insisted their relationship was a sham, but he knew she took life seriously. Was he subconsciously seeking something real?

When the song finished, Jen excused herself from her partner and went over to Eli.

"Dance with me?" she asked.

"I doubt you have any energy left, after all that jigging about you've been doing."

He'd been watching her...and he was even grumpier than before. Her heart swelled with tenderness. "I was getting in practice for you."

He grunted. "I guess we could dance."

Eli danced wonderfully, of course. Yet somehow Jen didn't feel clumsy as he led her through several fast numbers.

The band segued into a slow, romantic jazz tune. When Eli took Jen in his arms, she felt like a chicken who'd found a roost.

Dangerous thinking. But she indulged it anyway.

She relaxed against Eli, and felt a lessening of his top-to-toe tension.

"I watched you with those people, the charity clients," she said. "You were wonderful."

He made a sound of denial, but he held her closer. It was heaven, here in his arms. She gave herself up to the moment. Her head told her it wouldn't last. But her heart urged her to give him everything she could, just in case there was a chance they could make this real.

"You look beautiful tonight," he said gruffly. "I should have said earlier."

"Thank you."

His hand brushed her hip, then her derriere. Jen caught her breath.

"Let's get some air." His other hand tightened on her waist as he steered her through the crowd, out the French doors to a terrace. Along the railing, potted geraniums gave off a roselike scent. Beyond, the lights of uptown Charlotte glowed orange and red.

"Great view," Jen said, suddenly breathless.

"Amazing." Eli's eyes fixed on her mouth with an intensity that was incredibly flattering.

That was Eli, she reminded herself. Intense…for as long as the moment lasted.

He pulled her into his arms.

"Jen." His voice developed a heavy, curious quality that despite her total lack of experience with a man like him, some deep, inner part of her recognized.

"Yes," she said huskily. An instruction, not a question.

His eyes flared. His mouth came down on hers.

Jen felt as if her whole life, all twenty-two years, had been preparation for this moment. Preparation for the coaxing warmth of Eli's lips, for the possessive grasp of his hands. She shouldn't find this safe; it was the most dangerous thing she'd ever done…and yet underlying the adrenaline rush was a sense that this was *right*.

She parted her lips, welcomed him in…and the thrill got a whole lot more potent. Eli was all man: broad shoulders, strong arms and those oh-so-tempting lips. His hands roamed her curves, telling her how much he desired her.

She didn't want this kiss ever to end.

A flash of bright light startled her. Eli sprang away, lightning-quick.

"What the hell," he growled.

The photographer snapped another shot. "Sorry, folks, didn't mean to interrupt." He slipped his camera back into his bag in a hurry, perhaps recognizing Eli's intent to seek and destroy. "Tony Cinzano, *National Echo*. Any chance I could have the lady's name for my caption?"

Eli's snarl discouraged him from waiting around for an answer.

Jennifer tugged her bodice back into place, her fumbling fingers a marked contrast to the grace, the poetry of that kiss. "Blast," she muttered.

"No one with any sense reads that rag," Eli assured her.

"My grandfather doesn't, thank goodness," she agreed. "If you and I are going to do…this kind of thing I want him to find out about it from me, not some newspaper."

ELI WOULD HAVE LIKED to have enjoyed Jen's sweet taste a bit longer. He could slug that photographer, interrupting the best kiss of his—

It's been a while, that's all. A kiss is just a kiss.

But the kiss was over and, tactless though it seemed, coming on the heels of that sensuous encounter, Jen had just handed Eli the perfect opportunity to deliver his news about the change in status of their relationship.

He just needed to remember he was mad with her, so he could take the moral high ground, unfamiliar territory that he suspected she pretty much had staked out.

"We won't be *doing this kind of thing* again," he said.

Her hands stilled where they'd been adjusting one of the straps of her dress. "You sound very sure about that."

"You put my job in danger with that stuff you said to Gil this afternoon."

"You did that," she corrected him, "by going after a new job."

"You made things worse," he accused. "Who knows what that reporter will write?"

"It can't be worse than what she planned to write anyway."

Eli might have known she wouldn't give up without a fight. He had no choice but to be direct. "Jen, I'm ending our relationship."

She blinked. Then her hand went to her lips as if to confirm that, yes, the man who was now dumping her was the same one who'd kissed her a moment ago.

Eli shifted on his feet. "I shouldn't have kissed you," he said quickly. "But you were there and I was there...I seized the moment."

Her eyes narrowed. "Are you saying that's all that kiss was?"

"That's right." He sounded belligerent, so he toned it down. "Having you around will remind Gil how angry he is. The opposite of what I'm trying to achieve. The fake girlfriend routine isn't working anymore. So, it's over."

She stared at him for a long moment, then shook her head. "It's too late for that, Eli."

"What do you mean?" he asked.

"I care about you." And as if that wasn't bad enough, she added, "And you care about me."

Blood rushed at Eli's temples. "No, I don't."

"I know you like to keep your relationships short and saccharine-sweet," she said. "But all that fake sugar isn't good for you. You need to toughen up and try the real thing."

"I don't know what the hell you're talking about." But he was certain he didn't like it.

"You're afraid of being abandoned again," she said, "the way your family abandoned you, over and over. But it doesn't have to be like that."

A tight band constricted Eli's throat, he couldn't breathe. He tugged at his bow tie with both hands, and found air... just in time for Jen to land her sucker-punch.

"As of now, Eli, I'm your real girlfriend."

JEN HADN'T INTENDED TO SAY that at all. But somehow, she knew it was the right thing. Not that Eli *wanted* a real girlfriend—or at least, not that he knew it.

He safeguarded his heart by always having the Next Big Thing lined up, whether it was a house, a job or a woman. The loneliness that corroded his ability to stick with a relationship was deep-seated.

But she believed he wasn't beyond repair. That Eli had it in him to form regular relationships. To be, in that respect at least, an ordinary guy.

The horror on his face was almost comical.

"Jen," he warned.

She went up on tiptoe, planted a kiss on his mouth. As if she was entitled. He instinctively kissed her back, but cut it short with a scowl.

"If you *care* about me—" he threw her words back at him "—you'll give this up. I'm telling you, Gil doesn't want you around."

"And if I'm not around, you'll have those fans swarming

all over you again. Gil won't like that, either. I reckon at this stage he's pretty much a neutral factor in the equation."

"Okay, then, *I* don't want you around," he said. "You're a pain in the butt."

She recognized bluster when she saw it. "Right now, it's you and me against the world, Eli. Do you want it to be just you?"

He opened his mouth, so she hurried on before he said something he felt he couldn't back down on. "I think you and I could have something special, and I want you to give us a chance."

"You want a guy with a regular job, for Pete's sake!"

"I guess I can't have everything." She patted his hand. "If it's any consolation, this is downright dangerous for me, Eli. For an ordinary girl like me, dating you is like letting a fox into the henhouse."

"You're nuts." But the image must have appealed to him, because he ran his thumb along her bottom lip. She nipped the soft pad, and he growled, a low sound that made her stomach curl. "If you want to see some fox-in-henhouse action, just keep doing that," he dared her.

Reluctantly she pulled away. "This isn't about a physical relationship, Eli. Not yet. This is good, clean dating."

He made a sound reminiscent of steam coming out of a cartoon character's ears. "We're not dating. I don't want to date you."

The rejection stabbed, but Jen rallied and smiled. "Calm down, sweetie. Let's go dance some more. Then I might let you kiss me again."

Gil Sizemore wasn't the only person to notice a dazed Eli being led forcibly across the dance floor by a petite, determined woman. Jen only just managed to stifle her giggle.

CHAPTER TEN

By THE TIME ELI CALMED down enough to stop dancing with Jen—he had to find something to do with his hands, or else he'd strangle her—the crowd was starting to dwindle.

He'd put off going home, because it meant being alone with her and he was damned if he was going to listen to any more of her garbage about him being *abandoned*.

But the staff were cleaning up, and they couldn't stay. Jen retrieved her purse from the cloakroom and they headed for the door.

"Eli." Dixon Rogers called out. He beckoned to Eli.

"Wait here," Eli told Jen.

To his annoyance, she followed him.

"I owe you a phone call," Dixon said. "Might as well save myself the quarter."

He rearranged his troubled thoughts, found his smile. "Hi, Dixon." Reluctantly he introduced the Fulcrum Racing owner to Jen.

"I'm his girlfriend," Jen chirped.

Dixon smiled at her enthusiasm, then turned to Eli. "Our meeting on Wednesday…I've come to a conclusion."

Eli held his breath.

"I like the way you think, I like what you do on the track," Dixon said. "You've had a bad run lately, but you also have a flair that not many drivers share. Every guy out on that track is good, but only a handful have the air of a champion. To my mind, you're one of them."

"Thank you, sir." Eli felt almost as if he was blushing at such praise from a man who was one of his longtime heroes. He knew without a doubt that Dixon's next words would be a job offer. And he knew what he would say: yes. This would solve all his problems.

"Aargh." Jen clutched her stomach and doubled over.

"Are you all right?" Dixon's face crinkled with concern.

What the hell was she up to now?

"She's fine," Eli said. "You were saying?"

Jen gave a low moan. Dixon ignored Eli to focus on her. Which was exactly the reason for this little charade, Eli fumed. Not content with ruining his life with Gil, she was about to put the kibosh on his new job, too.

"I'm not sure," she panted, "maybe my appendix…"

"It's not your appendix," Eli said.

She squinted at him, and heaved a shuddering breath.

"She's really ill." Dixon grabbed Eli's arm. "You need to get her to a hospital."

"Dixon, she does this all the time…it's, uh, gas."

The expression on Jen's face was priceless, if only Dixon had been watching. He was too busy glaring in the face of Eli's lack of sympathy for his girlfriend.

"If you won't take her to the hospital, I'll call an ambulance," Dixon snapped.

Clearly he wasn't in any mood to go on discussing Eli's future. Quite the opposite—if Eli didn't start paying attention to his girlfriend's appendicitis, the offer of a ride with Fulcrum would likely evaporate.

"Okay, chickadee," he said through gritted teeth. "We'll get you checked out. Though I'm certain it's your gas problem flaring up again."

Jen's cheeks were pink with embarrassment and maybe the exertion of all that groaning she was doing. Eli was irritated to find her blush attractive. He wrapped an arm around her, gripping her shoulder with a force that said, *you're in trouble, lady,* and escorted her outside.

"HOW DARE YOU!" He rounded on her as soon as he had her in the car with the doors locked.

Jen clipped her seat belt, her stomachache miraculously healed. "You were about to tell Dixon Rogers you want to drive for him."

"Of course I was! He was offering me the job of my dreams...until you screwed it up," he added bitterly.

"What about Gil?" Jen asked.

Eli *pffed*. "What about him?"

"He gave you your first Cup ride. He backed you when no one else would, like you told that reporter."

"Were you there today when Gil said my job was hanging by a thread? When he told you to stay out of my business? How can you defend him?"

"I'm not defending him. Gil's acting like a jerk. That doesn't mean you don't owe him your loyalty."

Eli clutched his head. "This is NASCAR, not the Boy Scouts. There's no code of honor or fidelity pledge."

"I bet there is," she retorted. "Besides, Gil cares about you. That's why you two are fighting."

"Cares...are you kidding?" Eli jammed the key into the ignition. "NASCAR might run high on emotions, but it's not sentimental. I've had a good run at Double S, but nothing lasts forever."

"Loyalty matters," she said stubbornly. "Loyalty to more than yourself. Gil wants what's best for you, as well as the team. He wants you to get your act together. Far as I can see, not many other people in your life care that much."

He flinched, but came back fighting. "Dixon cares about

my future. He thinks I'm a champion in the making. And those guys at Fulcrum have a great time."

"That's important," she said sarcastically.

Why on earth had he expected her to understand, when she couldn't even grasp something as simple as *It's over?*

Eli started the engine and pulled out of the parking lot. "A smart driver is always lining up the next move in his career, just like he is on the track." He hesitated. "Just like he is with women." He'd forgotten to check out the talent tonight, he had so much on his mind, but he wasn't about to admit that.

She drew in a sharp breath, but he refused to feel guilty.

"Tomorrow I'm going to call Dixon and accept that ride. You and I—" he jabbed a finger at her "—are finished."

Jen spent the entire flight home, and the limo journey Eli had arranged to the farm, dissecting her new relationship.

Her one-sided relationship.

Despite her brave declaration to Eli that she was his real girlfriend and she wasn't going anywhere, reiterated even as he shoved her through the departure gate with obvious delight that he was rid of her, it was getting harder to convince herself she could make this work.

Yet she was certain she saw a deep longing inside Eli for someone who wouldn't leave, who would stick by him no matter what.

I could be that woman.

It was way too soon to think like that, of course. They barely knew each other. But that didn't stop her mind racing ahead, painting scenarios that involved a wedding and babies.

Maybe he was right: she was nuts.

When she arrived at the farm, the front door opened

without its familiar squeak. The guy Eli hired to help Granddad must have oiled it. "I'm home," she called.

"In the kitchen." Her grandfather's voice was strangely flat.

Jennifer's heart sped up. "Granddad?" She ran down the hallway. "Are you okay?"

She found him sitting at the kitchen table, a newspaper spread out in front of him. The *National Echo*.

She slowed her pace. "Since when do you buy that paper?"

He grunted. "Dennis Crane brought it over this morning. Thought I should see what a display my granddaughter is making of herself." He crumpled the page. "It made me feel sick."

"I—it can't be that bad." She and Eli had been kissing, that's all.

Carlton shoved the newspaper across the table. Jennifer sank into a seat. Two photos, one of her and Eli kissing. Okay, so his hands were on her butt rather possessively, but that wasn't too shocking.

The other photo was the one the guy had taken after they'd sprung apart. Eli looked annoyed, but very much in control of himself. Jennifer looked…a wreck. Her dress was lopsided, her hair disheveled, her mouth agape as if her brain had fallen out during that kiss.

"You look like a floozy," Carlton snapped.

"Anyone can take a bad photo," she said, trying not to cry.

"Your grandmother and I didn't raise you to chase after NASCAR drivers."

"He's a good man," Jennifer protested, her loyalty to Eli surging despite her own doubts. "Look how he arranged for help for you."

"Because he wants to get into your pants!" The crudeness

from a man who valued propriety shocked her. "Sweetheart, you don't watch NASCAR, so you don't know what I do about this guy," her grandfather said, more gently. "He grew up moving from pillar to post, he dates a different woman every week, he has a job you have to be downright crazy to do, no matter how much I enjoy watching those races."

She did know all that, and it didn't make any difference. Nor did it make a difference that the Internet search she'd carried out on his name had thrown up a dozen pictures of him kissing a dozen different women. Everyone had a past, so she couldn't hold that against him.

"Inside, he's a good man," she said again. Yet that photo summed up their relationship perfectly. Eli detached, in control, confident. Her eager, floundering, desperate.

"He doesn't know *how* to be a good man—leastways, not good enough for you," Carlton said. "I never thought you'd forget every blamed lesson you were ever taught."

Lessons not to make the kind of poor choices her parents had. Choices that had taken them away from home and ultimately from her.

"I admit Eli might look…flighty." She chose the word over more damning alternatives: unreliable, womanizing. "But every man settles down when he finds the right woman."

Her grandfather snorted. Which saved Jennifer the trouble. Even she could hear how pathetic she sounded, making excuses for a twenty-eight-year-old man who might never grow up.

CHAPTER ELEVEN

NOTHING LIKE A MORNING spent mucking out the chicken house to remind a girl that glamour is fleeting. By the time Jennifer arrived at work at eleven o'clock on Monday, her dreams had all but evaporated with the dew.

Why had she thought Eli could ever be serious about her? she wondered as she gave a family from Houston a tour of the track.

Then, at noon, his flowers arrived—an enormous bunch, some sort of lilies, exotically perfumed. Conscious of Bob Coffman's amused scrutiny, she pulled the card out of the little envelope.

"Sorry about the *Echo*," the message read.

So it wasn't exactly undying devotion. But he'd thought of her, known she'd be upset. Foolish hope glimmered. Maybe they weren't "finished."

Jen waited until she had some privacy, later in the day, to call Eli. "Thanks for the flowers…they're beautiful."

"They were Gil's idea," he said flatly.

"Oh." She quashed a pang of disappointment. And for the first time noticed he hadn't even put his name on the card. "Thank Gil for me, then. I have to admit I was horrified by those photos."

"Which just goes to show you're not the right girlfriend for me," he said. "That kind of press coverage is all part of the package. The women I usually date love seeing themselves in the media."

Which was enough to have her battle-ready again. "The women you usually date are disposable. I'm not."

He muttered something that might have been a curse.

"I've had a lot of flak from my grandfather about this," she said. "He must have given me two thousand reasons why I shouldn't date you."

"Smart man," Eli said. "And we're not dating. Though we do still have a business relationship—Gil expects to see you in Atlanta this weekend."

"I defended you," she told him calmly, ignoring his talk of business.

A short silence. "Who asked you to do that?" he said, with almost boyish defiance.

"Next time you send flowers," she said tartly, "make it your idea." She hung up on him.

Then she wondered, if Eli and Gil were still talking, did that mean he hadn't called Dixon Rogers yet? Or just that he hadn't told Gil?

ON TUESDAY, Eli sent team T-shirts and caps. "For the race at Atlanta," the card said. The size was perfect, the style more fitted than Jen normally wore. She had to admit, as she checked out her reflection in the bathroom mirror at work, the emerald-green color suited her.

She called Eli. "Whose idea was the clothing?"

"Mine," he admitted reluctantly. "But only because you'll need it for the race. I had the receptionist choose it—she's about your size."

In other words, Jen was interchangeable with any other women who happened to be at hand. But there was that note of defiance in his voice again, as if he was testing her.

"Not good enough," she said. "You're my boyfriend."

"I'm not your boyfriend," he growled.

"Why can't you be like an ordinary guy and buy me a personal, well-thought-out gift?" she asked.

This time, he hung up on her.

ELI COULDN'T BELIEVE a scrap of a girl like Jen was causing him so much grief. None of the women he dated questioned his gifts. If she thought he was about to spend some of his precious time choosing presents for her because she was his *girlfriend*, she was dreaming!

The only explanation for why he found himself looking at earrings in a jewelry store in Charlotte on Wednesday morning was that he appreciated the opportunity to argue with her.

He hadn't realized how hard it was keeping his carefree smile permanently in place until he'd let it slip with Jen. He relished the chance to gripe, to grumble, to fire insults.

I sound like her grandfather, he thought, appalled. Yeah, well, maybe people shouldn't wait until old age to say what they really thought. Jen certainly didn't.

Not that he was about to let go of what Jen would call his cover. He would keep up his happy-go-lucky persona with everyone else, and enjoy his conversations with her to the max.

Shame she couldn't get it out of her head that they should have a serious relationship. If he thought for a moment she could keep it casual, he'd take her to bed, make love to her all night. Then start all over again the next day, because one night wouldn't be enough to do all the things he wanted to—

Whoa! No way were he and Jen going near a bedroom. He'd have her feisty old grandfather coming after him with a rifle. Putting a bullet through his heart and plucking him like a chicken.

He'd have Jen expecting a ring on her finger.

Jen wasn't the kind of girl to fool around with. Bad, bad idea.

Eli inspected a pair of gold earrings, each drop comprising two gold balls, one on top of the other. He imagined them dangling from her little ears, saw them in his mind's eye next to the curve of her neck.

"I'll take these," he told the assistant, and gave delivery instructions.

JEN CALLED THURSDAY morning while Eli was in his office at home. He was startled at how his chest warmed to see her number on his cell phone. He kicked back in his chair, feet up on the desk, ready to receive her thanks.

"You really are an idiot," she said.

Dammit! His feet crashed to the floor. "I chose those earrings myself," he yelled. "I wrote the damn card myself." Okay, so maybe the message—*Thinking of you*—hadn't been that inspiring...

"I don't have pierced ears," she said. "You weren't *thinking of me* at all."

Eli found himself gaping at the phone. "Every woman I know has pierced ears."

"When will you learn that I'm not like the other women you've dated? You need to lift your game, Eli," she said haughtily.

Her turn to hang up.

Any other woman would be swooning with gratitude to have this much attention from him, whether she had pierced ears or not!

Eli tossed the cell phone onto the desk. It landed with a thud—the back fell off and the battery came out.

He couldn't believe he hadn't noticed that about Jen's ears. A real boyfriend ought to be ashamed of himself. *I'm not her boyfriend.*

He slapped the phone back together. Maybe he should buy her a necklace... She had a neck, didn't she? A damn stiff neck with a damn stubborn chin on top of it.

Eli brooded as he stared down at his phone. Tomorrow morning they would head to Atlanta for the race. Gil's PA had arranged flights for Jen. Eli was looking forward to seeing her. *To arguing with her and being every bit as blunt as she is.*

He wondered if she was so annoyed about the earrings she wouldn't turn up.

She would. She'd said she would and one thing about his Jen—*she's not my Jen*—she stuck with her promises. All that garbage about loyalty and so on.

Eli hoped she wasn't still trying to defend him to her grandfather, but he bet she was. He wondered if her loyalties were torn. Carlton was pretty special to her...

Eli thumbed the directory key on his phone and scrolled down to Kent Grosso's number.

AT EIGHT-THIRTY Friday morning, Jen finished mucking out the coop. She stripped off her gloves and washed her hands under the hose tap before heading inside—where she found Eli in the kitchen, pouring coffee from the pot she'd made earlier. Another man was there, too—handsome, but not as good-looking as Eli.

She dropped the gloves she'd planned to dump in the utility room.

"Morning, chickadee," Eli said.

"What are you doing here? How did you get in?"

"Your grandfather opened the door. Then he went to get dressed." He winked at her. "I wasn't expecting him to let me over the doorstep, but when he saw who I had with me..." He grinned at his companion.

"And you are?" Jen demanded.

The other man smiled. "My name's Kent Grosso, ma'am. It's a pleasure to meet you."

Kent Grosso? Granddad's favorite driver? Jen subsided into a seat at the table. "Why?" she asked Eli, her tone a whole lot less belligerent.

He shrugged. "Kent owed me a favor after I supported him in the draft at 'Dega."

"That's not what I mean."

Eli sighed, but he seemed to be enjoying himself. "Damned if I know. Maybe it'll get your grandfather off your back about those photos. He might even think I'm a decent guy."

And why, exactly, did he want Granddad to think he was a decent guy? Jen swallowed the bubble of hope and said acerbically, "More likely Kent will show you up."

Eli laughed. "Yeah, he does that. But it'll be the other way around out on the track."

Kent, a former NASCAR Sprint Cup Series champion, snorted.

"Shouldn't you be in Atlanta?" Jen asked.

Eli shrugged. "So long as we get there by eleven we'll be okay. We came in Kent's plane, so we're flexible. You can fly with us."

Her grandfather walked into the kitchen, rubbing his eyes as if he couldn't quite believe Kent was here, in his kitchen. The light in his face, his almost reverential expression, warmed Jen's heart.

She'd asked for a personal, well-thought-out gift, and Eli had done this for her.

"Mr. Ashby," Eli said, "I have to confess to an ulterior motive in bringing Kent here today."

"You're after my granddaughter," Carlton accused.

"No, sir."

Ouch.

"I'm after you giving her an easier ride," Eli said. "Your granddaughter is a woman of high integrity. She doesn't deserve to have you giving her trouble over her connection with me."

Right then, she forgave him for saying he wasn't after her.

Her grandfather fixed her with a gimlet stare. "That what she told you?"

"Of course not," Eli said. "She has nothing but good things to say about you, for some reason."

Jen gasped. Her grandfather barked a laugh. Kent folded his arms and watched the proceedings with interest.

"I suggest you trust Jen to do the right thing, the way you raised her," Eli said.

Carlton grunted. "Not always easy for a girl when there's a rapscallion like you turning her head."

"Jen's the strongest woman I know," Eli assured him.

He really believed that?

Eli held out a hand to Jen. "Let's go feed the chickens or something, let Kent and your granddad talk."

As they left the kitchen, she heard Granddad say, "Tell me about that time at Daytona when Justin Murphy put you into the wall on Turn Three."

Outside, they walked around to the front of the house. The sky seemed bluer than it had five minutes ago, the grass greener, the sun brighter. Could being with Eli do that? *Yes.*

"Was today's gift good enough?" Eli asked.

She stopped. "It was perfect. Thank you."

His eyes darkened as he took her in his arms.

His kiss, wonderful though it was, wasn't enough to drown out the thoughts clamoring in her head.

I love Eli. I'm in love with him.

It didn't make a lick of sense for a girl who was looking for an ordinary man to love Eli Ward.

But Jen did. She loved his outrageous NASCAR driver persona and his quiet, decent core. She loved his instinctive sensitivity to others' needs, the way he'd talked to the people at the charity gala, brought Kent to see her grandfather and intervened to make sure Granddad didn't give her a hard time. She loved that he called her on her conservative attitudes and sparked arguments that heightened her senses. She loved his sense of fun, his keen intelligence, his kisses... She loved him, and that was that.

Now she just had to convince him to love her back.

BY FRIDAY NIGHT, Eli had qualified third for Sunday's race in Atlanta, which had the whole team excited. Jen had hugged her feelings to herself all day, not wanting to break his concentration. Astute as he was, he'd looked at her once or twice with concern. "What's up, chickadee?" he asked at one stage. He looked so wary, she assured him everything was fine.

On Saturday, she and Eli were invited to Dean and Patsy Grosso's motor home for lunch, along with Kent and his wife, Tanya. The Grossos, Kent's parents and owners of Cargill-Grosso Racing, had heard about their son's visit to the chicken farm. They asked lots of interested questions about Jen and her grandfather.

They were so famous, so rich...but so nice and normal. This whole crazy world was starting to feel more comfortable to Jen. Sure, everyone flew around on private planes, and champagne corks popped on the slightest provocation. But these people were passionate about NASCAR, hardworking, yet dedicated to their families.

After lunch, Jen helped Patsy and Tanya with the dishes. Which turned out to be an excuse for them to ask her all kinds of personal questions while the men watched a season opener football game on TV.

"So what's the scoop with you and Eli?" Tanya asked. "I've never actually met one of his girlfriends before. It's always been a case of blink and you miss 'em."

"Tanya!" Patsy laughed. "Not so loud." She took a stack of dry plates from Jen and put them in a cupboard.

"They can't hear us," Tanya said. She was right—the game was obviously reaching some kind of peak, because the guys were yelling encouragement at the TV set.

"I'm not sure Eli would describe me as a girlfriend," Jen said.

"You're much more than that," Patsy suggested.

"I—no—I don't know." Jen knew she was blushing. Behind her, the guys rose to their feet, urging some football player on.

"Do you love him?" Tanya asked eagerly, her dish-drying forgotten.

Was this how all celebrities talked? Sure, they'd gotten along well over lunch, but expecting a near stranger to bare her heart? "I don't think—" Jen began.

"You do!" Tanya crowed. "It's written all over your face." Groans came from behind them and the men subsided onto the couch in defeated silence, just as Tanya squealed, "You're in love with Eli!"

She clapped a hand over her mouth.

Too late.

There was only so far sound had to travel to reach every corner of a motor home, and Tanya's words had gone the distance.

The TV must have still been on, but all Jen heard was the horrified silence. All she saw was Eli's back, rigidly turned against her. No way was he ready to hear she loved him—he was still fighting the idea of having a proper girlfriend.

If Jen had been the kind of woman Eli liked to date, she'd have pulled out a witty, flirtatious remark and laughed the whole thing off. Then proceeded to show Eli such a good time in bed, he'd forget all about her inconvenient feelings for him.

But she was ordinary Jen Ashby and this was the first time she'd been in love and she had no idea what to do.

She turned on her heel and ran out of the motor home.

As HE CHECKED HIS HELMET and pulled on his gloves behind the wheel of the No. 502 car, Eli was certain this race would be a disaster. He'd lucked out at Bristol, running well despite his preoccupation. But back then—it seemed like months ago, not two short weeks—he'd been dealing with a slightly kooky fake girlfriend. Not a woman who was in love with him and who doubtless, being the kind of woman she was, wanted to dig deep into his psyche to find some pathetic guy desperate enough to tie himself down.

He'd been furious when Jen ran off from the Grossos', leaving him to explain that Tanya had it all wrong. They hadn't believed him. He hadn't believed it, either. *This* was why Jen had been withdrawn since he showed up at the farm with Kent. She'd decided she loved him.

What the hell was he supposed to do about that?

He'd phoned her hotel room to give her a chance to laugh it off, so they could get back to their flirting and kissing and arguing.

"It's not as if you and I are even dating, chickadee," he'd teased her down the line, ignoring the dampness in her voice. "We barely know each other." He also ignored the fact that he felt as if he knew her better than any woman he'd dated. "You gotta wonder if Tanya's been sniffing Kent's fuel cell."

There it was, the point where Jen could set his mind at

rest. She just had to say Tanya Grosso was crazy, and he would accept it as gospel. They would never mention this again.

In the long silence that ensued, he remembered how damn honest she was.

"I'm not going to lie to you, Eli," she said. "I love you."

He whipped the phone away from his ear and stared at it. She'd just ruined everything!

She was saying something; he listened again.

"—think you could love me back, you and I could have a real relationship, if you would just be brave enough to—"

"I'm not *afraid,*" he cut in, his heart hammering like a piston. "What I've been trying to tell you, as long as I've known you, is that I like my life just fine. There's nothing missing." He paused. "Jen, I'm not going to love you back."

Having made that point, he'd been surprised—and disturbed—to see her in the hauler this morning. Thankfully she'd greeted him calmly, even if her reddened eyes hadn't met his.

Then he'd realized she was here because he was paying her, and the thought had unreasonably annoyed him.

All day, she'd done her job—kept the female fans away from him—while barely exchanging any words with Eli. Since Gil wasn't talking to him, either, it made for a quiet day. See, this was the problem with relationships. The more time you spent with someone, the more they started taking stuff personally and the harder it was to move on painlessly.

I must phone Dixon Rogers tomorrow. The week had been so busy, with all that damn gift-buying for Jen, he hadn't gotten around to calling the Fulcrum boss yet.

"Gentlemen," the Grand Marshal announced over the PA system, "start your engines."

Eli hit the No. 502's starter button. The engine's hungry, throaty roar surrounded him, reminding him nothing mattered more than this.

He pulled out of his pit stall and ruthlessly banished Jen's reddened eyes from his mind.

JEN HAD THOUGHT SHE WOULD have no interest in the race after Eli dismissed her from his life with the exact same ease as he'd dismissed every other woman.

She hadn't expected him to react well to her confession that she loved him, but the finality in his voice when he'd declared he wasn't going to love her back had sent a shaft of pain through her. It reduced her to tears, a luxury she seldom indulged in.

Then she'd gotten mad, so mad she could barely speak to him. Okay, so he struggled with emotional commitment. But did he have to be such a coward?

Jen sighed. Even if Tanya hadn't been so indiscreet, Eli would have figured out eventually that she loved him. This was something they'd have had to go through sooner or later. His harsh reaction was a product of his fear. Maybe, when he got used to the idea, he'd realize being loved wasn't so bad. Maybe he'd even want to give loving her a try. He just needed space to process his feelings.

The No. 502 car came into focus on the TV set at the base of the pit box. As she watched, Eli passed Kent Grosso, then Ben Edmonds. He was driving rather well—her inexpert assessment was backed up by the comments from some of the pit crew.

He continued to drive well, exploiting his advantageous starting position and staying at the front of the pack. At the end of the five-hundred-mile race, Eli was first over the line.

His first NASCAR Sprint Cup Series win!

An impromptu party sprang up right there in the pits. Gil, back from the Victory Lane media frenzy ahead of Eli, brought Jen a beer.

"Thanks." Recognizing a peace offering, she took it.

He clinked his bottle against hers. "That was one hell of a drive. I want to thank you for the help you've been to Eli."

"I haven't done anything," she said.

"That's not true. Since he met you he's been focusing on the right things." Gil took a swig of his beer. "I expected to see you in Victory Lane. Did you two have a fight?"

"Something like that," Jen said.

"Not too serious, I hope," Gil said. "Eli has a much better chance of making the Chase after today, but he'll still need to give next week's race everything he's got. He'll need the same focus he had today, and then some."

The following Saturday was the race at Richmond, the final decider for the Chase contenders.

A cheer rose from the team as Eli arrived in Victory Lane. Smiling widely, green eyes alight with triumph, he looked impossibly gorgeous. He accepted the accolades of his team, and dealt them right back again, acknowledging each individual's contribution to today's race with a graciousness that suggested he was a born winner.

Jen stayed a good ten feet away from him, near enough that people wouldn't suspect the rift between them, but not so close that he could snub her.

A woman—dark-haired and gorgeous—approached him. Her midriff-baring black T-shirt bore the logo of First Rate Auto Loans, Will Branch's sponsor.

"Eli, you were incredible today," she said breathlessly.

She laid a hand on Eli's arm, leaned in close enough for him to get a good eyeful of her curves.

Jen tensed.

"Thanks." Eli pulled away, as he instinctively did when people got too close.

The woman stayed in his space. "You don't remember me, do you?" Her lips pouted sexily. "I'm Kylie. We met in Talladega in April."

The way she emphasized *met,* it was clear she and Eli had done more than just talk. Jealousy punched Jen in the stomach, then for good measure took a hold of her gut and twisted. She could scarcely breathe.

Her only consolation was Eli's hunted look. He glanced around, seeking escape, and met Jen's eyes.

She couldn't help it: her love for him welled up, overflowed into a smile.

Eli stiffened. Then he said to the dark-haired beauty, "Kylie, gorgeous, as if I could forget you."

It was all the encouragement Kylie needed. She threw her arms around him and kissed him. Eli's gaze held Jen's for a fraction of a second. Then he kissed Kylie back. Long and hard.

A red haze of fury clouded Jen's vision. She stomped over to Eli, as his team members scrambled to the far side of the pit stall, out of the way of looming embarrassment.

"You *coward*," she said.

Eli let go of Kylie. Shame flashed across his face. Then he registered what she'd called him. He donned that superficial, charm-loaded smile and said, "Hey, chickadee, Kylie here was just congratulating me on my win."

Jen thumped the heel of her hand into his chest, taking him by surprise. He stumbled back a step.

"You lily-livered *jackass*," she said. "Are you seriously

going to pass up the chance for a real, lasting love just because you're scared to take a *risk?*"

Awkward murmurs rose behind her. Kylie gave Jen a pitying look. Clearly she wasn't the kind of woman who'd make the mistake of telling a guy like Eli she loved him.

Eli's face darkened. "I take risks every time I get in my race car. You're the one who's stuck in a rut because you're afraid to live life to the fullest."

"You can't live life to the fullest if you can't love," Jen retorted. "Falling in love with you was a king-size risk, but I took it. Now I want you to stop hiding behind women like Kylie—" the other woman hissed her displeasure "—and take a chance on loving me back. Come on, Eli, seize the day. Seize *love*."

She put everything she felt for him into her eyes as she beseeched him. And saw pure terror looking back.

No, not pure terror. There was something else in those green eyes, something Jen chose to interpret as longing.

Silence stretched between them.

She'd said her piece; she wasn't about to beg. She didn't need a pledge of undying commitment from Eli. Just a commitment to try.

Kylie wound her arm through Eli's, pressed herself against him. "If you're done here, we could go celebrate at my place," she suggested.

Eli glanced down at her, then back at Jen.

The choice couldn't be clearer, she thought. A roll in the hay with Kylie that he'd have forgotten by next week, or a relationship with Jen that would demand hard work, but which might make him happier than he knew he could be.

Seize the day, Eli. Seize *me*.

She saw the moment he made his decision, the moment the shutters came down, leaving his expression bland.

"Sure," he said to Kylie. "I'm done here."

CHAPTER TWELVE

"Thirty minutes," Kevin Horton called across the garage at Richmond.

Eli acknowledged the reminder with the lift of a hand. Soon he'd be in the car and it would be down to him, and no one else, if he didn't make the Chase. His chances were better now than they'd been a couple of weeks ago, but it was still by no means certain. Which was why he'd spent hours in the gym this week, putting himself through the grueling cardio workouts that would get him into great physical shape for tonight's race.

Too bad his mental shape was shot to bits.

He'd turned Jen down last week, called an end to a relationship that would demand far more than he had to give. He'd expected to feel free, off the hook of her demands. But the moment Jen had walked away, he'd realized he had no interest in Kylie, no interest in any other woman. Jen had taken up residence in every nook and corner of his mind, and he couldn't process a single damn thought without her intruding.

Worse, the prospect of weeks, then months, then years without her stretched before him, an endless vista of, dammit, loneliness. He'd sent her away, but he felt as if she'd abandoned him.

Which was crazy, given she was right here, standing outside the hauler, talking to Gil.

Eli hadn't invited her. When he arrived home from

Atlanta he'd sent her a check for ten thousand dollars, along with a note to say he didn't need her at Richmond. Gil wasn't about to fire him after his first win, and the Rev Energy Drinks sponsorship was no longer in danger. Eli had confessed to Gil that he'd asked Jen to act as his girlfriend so he could keep his job and Gil had forgiven him.

Gil was the one who'd decided Eli couldn't focus on his racing without Jen around to keep women away. He'd asked her come to Richmond as a personal favor to him.

His ex-girlfriend and his boss were best buddies these days. That profile of Double S Racing in the *Observer* had been glowing, and Gil credited Jen for much of the positive coverage. He was even talking of offering her a job at team headquarters.

Eli's stomach hollowed at the thought of seeing her every day and not being able to kiss her.

I need to get out, start dating again. He didn't want to. Couldn't imagine being with anyone other than Jen.

Maybe they could go back to where they'd been. Sort-of dating, but not really. So he could see her, argue with her, kiss her, but not have to actually commit to her.

Even he could see she'd be stupid to settle for that. He'd made his choice, and he'd just have to get over her.

Gil approached, Jen at his side. "Time to head over the wall, Eli," he said.

"Uh, right." Eli could barely remember why he was here, he was so caught up in looking at Jen. She wasn't wearing anything fancy—jeans, T-shirt, ball cap, as usual. But she was the most beautiful woman he'd ever seen.

"Will you come with me?" he asked her.

"Sure." Her voice was neutral, as it had been all weekend, even when he'd told her he hadn't gone to Kylie's place, hadn't done anything at all with her. Jen hadn't seemed to care, and Eli had told himself that if she was falling out of love with him that was a good thing.

Though it was night, it was bright as day in the pits. Eli's success last week meant he had a lot more media attention on him. He knew the photographers wanted their shot of him kissing Jen before he climbed into the car, but he was too ashamed of the way he'd behaved to ask her to cooperate.

Turned out he didn't need to ask. Jen stepped up to him, as if he was still paying her to act as his girlfriend.

Eli put his arms around her and it felt like the best thing he'd done all week. In her brown eyes, he saw a purity and a permanence that he'd never wanted before, but which suddenly he craved.

No, I don't. What if I fell for Jen and then changed my mind? It would hurt her. What if she changed her mind and left?

She's already left. Because I acted like an idiot and drove her away.

He froze, as pain shafted through him, down through layer upon layer of the carefree life he'd constructed, right into his soft, vulnerable core.

It hurt so bad, he couldn't breathe.

"Eli?" Jen shifted in his arms. "Drive safely." She went up on tiptoe, pressed her lips to his. She was out of his embrace before he could tell her what he'd just realized.

He loved her.

AFTER A LONG, HOT RACE, Eli swept over the finish line in third place. More than good enough to secure his position in the Chase.

As if he gave a damn. He had to find Jen, right now.

"You did it." Gil punched his shoulder, then gave him a hug. "Congratulations, Eli."

"Where's Jen?" Eli scanned the pits.

"She's around somewhere. How about we all go out for dinner?"

Eli said something noncommittal as he vaulted the wall. He headed to the hauler. Jen wasn't there.

Back outside, he combed the crowd with his eyes. It was much darker here than in the pits.

Dixon Rogers came up. "Eli, great drive."

"Thanks," Eli said distractedly.

"It's time we talked turkey about you driving for us," Dixon said. That did catch his attention. "Bring your crew chief with you, if you like," Dixon continued.

"Really?" Eli said. Having Kevin with him would make a big difference.

Dixon smiled. "I think you'll find our terms favorable." He named a salary that made Eli's head spin. "If you're interested, my lawyers and yours can meet on Monday to start hammering out a deal."

It was the deal of his dreams, with the team of his dreams. Eli almost blurted out a yes then and there.

Then he heard a soft but determined voice in his head. Jen. Talking about loyalty and commitment.

But there's no such thing as commitment in NASCAR, he argued with her in his mind.

And realized he was wrong. The spirit of NASCAR was enduring, the sport had survived all kinds of setbacks to be still going, sixty-some years after that first race. That must have taken one hell of a lot of commitment by a whole bunch of people.

"What do you say?" Dixon asked.

Eli took a deep breath and let go of one dream in the interest of holding on to another he was only just realizing he held. The dream of being a man who could make a relationship last. "I'm honored to be asked, but Gil and Double S are home for me."

And contrary to what Eli had told Jen when she'd visited his house, home wasn't overrated.

"Dixon, you haven't seen Jen, have you?" he asked, interrupting Dixon's expression of regret.

"Matter of fact I ran into her a few minutes ago," Dixon said. "She was on her way out, said she wanted to get to the taxi line ahead of the rush."

Jen was leaving? Just when he'd found something worth sticking around for? Something worth fighting for?

"I gotta go," Eli said.

CHAPTER THIRTEEN

JEN CLIMBED INTO THE taxi feeling as bereft as Cinderella must have leaving the ball. She would see Eli again if she took the job Gil had offered her, but tonight felt like the severing of their personal ties. He'd made the Chase, and now he would go on without her.

When she'd kissed him before the race she'd seen in his eyes that he cared about her. But she no longer believed he had it in him to get over the hurts of his past. Out on the race track, he was fearless, but in his heart…

As she reached for her seat belt she saw Eli crossing the pavement, looking right at her. Her heart leaped. Then a woman, a gorgeous blonde, stepped in front of him. She appeared to be gushing about his race. Two other women waited their turn behind the blonde.

It was like a replay of that first time they met, in the garage at Bristol. This was the way it would always be for him.

She clicked her seat belt. "The airport," she told the driver.

As the cab pulled out, she didn't look back.

Which was why the sudden wrenching open of the door startled her so badly. She shrieked as Eli threw himself into the car.

"You idiot. You could have been killed," she yelled.

"Not me, chickadee." He had the nerve to wink at her.

"Stop the car," he told the driver. He grabbed Jen's hand. "We have some celebrating to do."

"There are a thousand other women out there who'd love to celebrate your result." She freed her hand from his. "Drive on," she ordered.

"It's not my race I want to celebrate," he said cryptically. "But you're right, we need somewhere special. Take us to the fanciest restaurant in town," he instructed the driver.

The guy flipped his turn signal from left to right.

"The airport," Jen told him firmly. "That's where I'm going."

With a sigh, the driver turned left onto the expressway.

"There's a NASCAR museum around here somewhere," Eli said. "Maybe I can convince them to open specially for us."

Jen would bet he could. He radiated excitement, and it made him even more compelling than usual. She realized with a pang of regret that he must have accepted the ride with Fulcrum Racing. He was moving on from Double S, just like he was moving on from her.

The driver slowed, clearly expecting another redirection.

"I'm going to the airport," Jen snapped. "If you want to celebrate, go back to those women you were flirting with back there."

Eli started to laugh. "Dammit, Jen, I'm trying to find somewhere special so I can tell you I love you!"

The world spun around her. The taxi swerved in sympathy, the driver obviously equally shocked.

"What did you say?" she whispered.

"I love you, Jen." He brought her hand to his lips, kissed her knuckles with a tenderness that melted her heart. "I know you might take some convincing after the jerk I've been, but in my defense, I'm only just figuring what it's all about."

"What *what's* all about?" she asked, unable to believe he could love her the same way she loved him. Did he mean he wanted a fling with her?

"Commitment," he said. "I've made a start, but I've got a long way to go." Then he told her Fulcrum Racing had made him an incredible offer, but he'd turned it down to stay with Gil.

"I realized some things are meant to last," Eli said. "Like you and me. You're so deep inside me, like nothing else has ever has been, this is forever."

A glorious hope suffused her, left her speechless.

He froze. "That is, if you still love me. If I haven't screwed this up completely. Have I?" he asked, the words an agonized groan.

Jen couldn't stand to see him lonely or vulnerable for another moment…but she checked her impulse to throw her arms around him and declare her love. Because Eli might think he loved her now and for always. But what if he changed his mind?

Terror engulfed her…a flood of fear. Suddenly she knew exactly how he'd been feeling.

"Jen?" Eli shook her hands. "Sweetheart, please, talk to me."

"I love you, Eli—" he reached for her, but she put up a warning hand "—but we have a lot of things to work out."

"What things?" he demanded.

She didn't want to tell him she was worried he'd change his mind. "My grandfather, for one. He won't be happy about me rushing into this. Maybe we should take it slowly."

ELI HADN'T COME SO FAR, so fast to put the brakes on now.

"Chickadee, no way am I giving you time to figure out you could do much better than a guy like me." He pulled his cell phone from his pocket. "Watch this." A moment later he was talking to her grandfather. "Mr. Ashby, this is Eli Ward."

"What time do you call this?" the old man barked.

Damn. "Uh, yes, it is late, sir, and I'm sorry about that, but this can't wait. I'm in love with Jen and I want to marry her."

Jen gaped—had he forgotten to mention the part about marrying her? He flashed her a cocky grin.

"We'd like your blessing," he said to her grandfather.

There was a pause.

"I didn't raise my granddaughter to have her head turned by some hotshot NASCAR driver who'll break her heart," Carlton snapped.

"Mr. Ashby, I won't—"

"So you can damn well keep your hands off her!"

No fair. Eli hadn't even had his hands on her yet!

"Sir, I promise I'll do everything I can to make her happy."

It was no use. Carlton had worked up a head of steam and he ranted down the phone without pause, making it clear that if he had his way, Eli would never, ever marry Jen.

Then Jen took the phone from him. "Granddad? I love Eli, and I always will," she said, soft enough that her grandfather would have to stop blustering so he could hear. "He's a good man, a forever kind of man."

Words that should have made Eli want to run. Instead he was proud, prouder than he'd ever been at the end of a race. Jen saw him as a forever kind of guy!

"Yes, I know it's a risk," she told Carlton. "But it's a tiny one, and the reward is so much greater. I plan to marry Eli."

Eli's heart started thumping.

"I plan to have children with him eventually." She shot Eli a querying look and he gave her a thumbs-up. He'd never thought about kids, but now he wanted them with Jen—not right away, but one day. Right now, he'd settle for getting his hands on her and making slow, passionate love to her. "So I'd very much like the blessing of those children's great-grandfather," she told Carlton.

He could still hear her grandfather sputtering, though less aggressively, when she ended the call. She collapsed into laughter.

"I just about had a heart attack!" Eli complained. "What's so funny?"

She wiped her eyes. "You, so convinced that your incredible charm could sway my grandfather."

"It swayed you," he pointed out, then started laughing, too. He loved laughing with her. He swept her into his arms and vowed to himself they would always laugh. Then he kissed her.

When he lifted his head, the taxi was pulling up outside the airport terminal, seething with departing NASCAR fans and media. They got out, and Eli paid the driver.

"Where shall we go?" he asked Jen. "I want to propose to you properly."

"The best place for me is wherever you are."

His heart swelled. "You're right, as always." He dropped to one knee, right there in front of the crowd.

"Eli!" she squawked.

He took her hands in his, looked up at the sweet, beautiful face he would never tire of. "Jennifer Ashby, you're a woman in a million. The only woman for me. Will you marry me?"

"Yes," she said, and drew him to his feet for what just became the best kiss of his life.

* * * * *

Daisy Chain

Marisa Carroll

To Marsha Zinberg, Tina Colombo and Stacy Boyd—
thanks for inviting us along for a great ride!

CHAPTER ONE

DAISY BROOKSHIRE HELD the faded, rainbow-striped umbrella above her head and walked slowly uphill toward the line of granite markers at the top of the gentle slope. Her grandmother, a stickler for etiquette, would have frowned on the frivolous choice of rainbow stripes to visit a gravesite, but it was the only umbrella Daisy owned and she wasn't about to spend any of her small savings on a black one.

Her baby's father lay beneath the largest of those monuments. Her heart thudded heavily in her chest as she drew close enough to read the name and dates chiseled into the ebony stone. She hadn't gone to Brendan Carlyle's funeral, or even his wake. She wouldn't have been welcomed there. She probably shouldn't even have come here today. What if she ran into Brendan's father or stepmother? She had successfully avoided the wealthy couple for the past few months but she didn't delude herself that they had given up trying to coerce her into giving up her child—Brendan's baby. But she couldn't stay away. She had to risk this one short visit, some small, still-grieving part of her needed to see his tombstone, needed to face the awful finality of his death.

Oakhill Cemetery was a beautiful place to spend eternity, she supposed, but not when you came to your small portion of it six months shy of your twenty-fifth birthday.

Daisy halted, taking a moment to catch her breath. It was an unusually cool August afternoon in Concord, North Carolina, still and quiet all around her, the sound of raindrops hitting the leaves of the live oaks that gave the cemetery its name, muting the rumble of distant traffic on the busy highway beyond the stone and wrought-iron fence. The hillside wasn't particularly steep, but when you were eight and a half months pregnant even getting out of bed in the morning could cause you to lose your breath. She stared down at the wet ground beyond her swollen belly—her feet had disappeared from view weeks ago—and contemplated turning around and going back to Cut 'N' Chat, the Mooresville, North Carolina, beauty salon where she felt most at home.

Instead she began climbing again, still looking at the ground. Turning tail and running back to the familiarity of Rue Larrabee's salon was out of the question. She needed to say her goodbyes to the handsome, high-spirited, selfish young man she had thought was the love of her life—until he told her, while he cared for her, he wasn't about to marry her and more than likely be disinherited by his wealthy father— even if she was carrying his child. He'd support their baby financially, but he wasn't ready to settle down. They would work something out later, after he'd broken the news to his parents. Then he'd jetted off to Bermuda with his father and stepmother, leaving Daisy brokenhearted and three months pregnant. Six days later he was dead, the victim of a freak paragliding accident.

She had gone to ground since Brendan's death, working quietly at the salon that catered to a number of NASCAR drivers' and team members' wives and sisters and daughters, but her conscience—and her heart—insisted she seek out his resting place and say her last goodbye. He had betrayed her trust and broken her heart but he was still her baby's father. She squared her shoulders and lifted her eyes to the granite marker the lady at the old-fashioned gatehouse office had given her directions to and found she was not the only mourner at Brendan Carlyle's grave. A tall, dark-haired man in a gray suit, head bowed, blocked her path.

Expensive suit. Italian shoes. Money. One of August Carlyle's minions? A lawyer, possibly. One of the high-priced, high-powered attorneys that kept sending her letters demanding she give Brendan's father access to her child or suffer the consequences—consequences never spelled out and all the more terrifying for their vagueness. She wondered if she could somehow turn and hurry back down the hill without being seen, but she knew that wasn't possible. The moment he looked up he would see her standing there staring at him, look at her pregnant belly and know who she was. And of course that was exactly what happened. He raised his head. His hair was the color of midnight, his skin bronzed by the sun, but his eyes when they met hers were a clear and startling blue. There was a bump on his nose from a long-ago injury and a scar at the corner of his left eye.

She knew, suddenly, how he'd come by those injuries— and a broken collarbone, as well—falling out of a tree trying to rescue his little brother, Brendan, who had climbed high into the branches to try to touch a cloud.

"Daisy?" he asked, a frown pulling his dark eyebrows together over those startling blue eyes.

She responded with a question of her own. "Are you Brendan's brother?" She was shaking so hard she had to clutch the umbrella handle with both hands to keep it from shaking, too. Brendan had idolized Quinn Parrish. He had talked about him constantly during the time they were together, even though Quinn had had little or nothing to do with the Carlyle family since he'd left home when Brendan was thirteen.

"Stepbrother," he clarified and his voice was hard when he spoke the word. Quinn, who was in his early thirties, was the owner and CEO of Parrish Commodities, the makers of Rev Energy Drinks and sponsor of Double S Racing's No. 502 car in the NASCAR Sprint Cup Series. "You're

Daisy Brookshire, aren't you?" It wasn't really a question, more like a command to respond.

"I'm Daisy." Daisy was her nickname. Her father had given it to her when she was small. Her real name was Deidre. She never used it. No one did—except August Carlyle's lawyers.

"You weren't at the funeral," he said straightforwardly. "I would have remembered you." He wasn't wearing a hat. Raindrops beaded in his dark hair like diamonds but he seemed oblivious to the weather.

"I didn't think I would be welcome." Her voice broke despite her best efforts to keep it even and steady. The baby moved restlessly inside her and it took all her willpower not to cup her hand protectively over her swollen stomach.

"I know the feeling." He turned his head and looked at the monument again. His stance was easy, relaxed, but Daisy saw him swallow hard and knew he was far more moved than he appeared to be. "He was a good kid."

She nodded. It was all she could manage. Brendan hadn't been good to her, not at the end. Quinn continued to stare down at his brother's grave and she continued to watch him, her wariness of the living much stronger than her grief for the dead and gone. But she had to be careful what more she said. Just because Quinn Parrish was estranged from the older Carlyle didn't mean he still didn't pose a threat to her and her baby.

Any man who could take a small, barely-breaking-even regional soft-drink bottler and in five years parlay it into a brand of energy drinks known round the world was a force to be reckoned with. For a fleeting moment she wished that some of this man's drive and ambition had transferred itself onto her baby's father. Maybe then everything would be different. Brendan wouldn't be dead and she wouldn't be afraid for herself—and her baby's future.

"Was my brother going to do the right thing and marry you?" he asked.

The unexpectedness of the question surprised her into answering just as bluntly as he had spoken. "No."

"Damned fool," he said, but his voice was gruff with suppressed emotion. "Did he make any financial provisions for you and the baby?"

"No."

"What about my stepfather and my mother? Are they helping you?"

"No." He might not know about the Carlyles wanting custody of her baby. He had been out of the country for over a year. The age-old fight or flight instinct urged her to flee for her baby's sake. "I don't want anything from Brendan's family. Nothing. I'll do fine on my own. Look…I have to go. I have to get back to work." Foolish. She had let herself be lulled by this man's sorrow for his lost brother. He was still a Carlyle, if not by blood then by marriage. He was as big a threat to her as August Carlyle himself.

The baby moved again, increasing her anxiety. The rain had begun to come down in earnest now. She started backing away. "My condolences on your loss."

"Wait." Quinn held out his hand. He had to know more about her. Daisy Brookshire had been nothing more than a name attached to a photograph his brother had e-mailed him. He had recognized her honey-blond hair, her heart-shaped face and stubborn chin the moment he spotted her, but he hadn't realized how small she was in real life, how fragile-looking. She was young, too, about Brendan's age, seven or eight years his junior.

Brendan hadn't told him she was pregnant. Maybe he hadn't known himself when he sent the picture, Quinn thought, casting back through his memories to pinpoint the date the photo had shown up in his e-mail. He hadn't learned she was carrying his dead stepbrother's child until a week ago when his mother had told him. In the days since then he'd been debating whether to try to contact her or not. Now the decision had been made for him when fate had chosen to bring them both together over Brendan's grave.

She was a stranger but she was carrying Brendan's child and that made her important to him. He hadn't been able to save his little stepbrother when he fell out of the sky a second time but he wasn't about to let the mother of his child disappear out of his life as suddenly as she had appeared. "Daisy, wait. We need to talk."

She stopped backing away and stood stiff and still. "I have to get back to work," she said.

"Did you love my brother?"

She turned pale beneath the soft golden tan of her skin, but looked him straight in the eye when she replied. "I thought I did." He admired her honesty.

"He would have come around, Daisy. He was a good kid. He was just spoiled and immature." He spoke the truth as well, but he wondered how long it would have taken for Brendan to become his own man. Far longer than this young but determined woman would have waited, he suspected.

"I'd like to think you're right for his daughter's sake, but we'll never know, will we?"

"The baby's a girl?"

"Yes."

"Brendan would have been happy about that. I have a picture of the two of you—" His voice faltered for a moment. "My brother e-mailed it to me a couple of weeks before his death. You were sitting in front of a fireplace. His arms were around you. You looked happy."

"We were happy," she said. "We went skiing in Colorado. I had never been out west, never seen the mountains. I told him about the baby just after that picture was taken." Her lips tightened and a flicker of anger and hurt flashed behind her eyes. "We…we were never that happy together again."

And six weeks later his brother had died, leaving Daisy and their unborn child to fend for themselves.

"Daisy, we can't keep standing here in the rain. Let me take you somewhere we can—"

She shook her head. "No. I already told you I don't want anything to do with Brendan's family." She tipped her head back, lifted her chin, her voice was steady, her tone implacable. "That includes you." She turned on her heel and started down the gentle incline toward the graveled lane that wound among the older headstones.

"Wait." He started after her. He had no idea where she lived or how to contact her. He couldn't just let her walk away. His mother had told him she would have nothing to do with her or her husband. He didn't blame Daisy for that: August was a hard, old bastard, but she was carrying his brother's child and she wasn't going to be rid of him so easily. "Daisy, wait," he called again.

She flung up her free hand, shook her head and began to run, an awkward little jog. He sucked in his breath. Should she be doing that when she was so far along? What if she tripped and fell? He wanted to holler at her to slow down, to stop and wait for him to give her a hand where the roots of the old oaks had heaved up through the ground, but she just kept going, fighting to close the incongruous rainbow-striped umbrella as she ran. He followed her down the hill, staying far enough back so that she didn't catch sight of him out of the corner of her eye.

She headed for a beat-up sedan parked at the base of the slope. He'd left his SUV another hundred yards closer to the entrance; she'd have to pass him to get out of the gate. He slowed his pace, knowing that by the time she followed the narrow, winding driveway to the nearest cul-de-sac so that she could turn her car around, he would be able to intercept her, and hopefully get her to agree to talk with him about the baby's future, and her own, somewhere warm and dry. But he miscalculated her determination, and her driving ability.

While Quinn watched in consternation she got into the ancient car and began backing toward the entrance gate. He hadn't expected her to do something like that. He broke into a trot keeping one eye on the treacherous footing and one eye on Daisy. "I'll be damned," he said under his breath as she maneuvered expertly along the narrow driveway. "Where'd she learn to drive like that?" Then again this was the heart of NASCAR country and home base for a lot of NASCAR Sprint Cup teams. Why wouldn't she know how to drive better than most?

He didn't have any more time for speculation. She arrowed past his big black SUV and wheeled the sedan onto the concrete apron that paralleled the stone wall inside the main gate. Quinn sprinted for his car. He pushed the button on his key ring and the SUV's engine roared to life. He was close enough now to see Daisy's face through the windshield. Her eyes met his for a second and panic flared in their golden-brown depths.

"Damn." This time the curse was for himself. He'd scared her and that was the last thing he'd wanted to do. Old August and his lawyerly threats must have really done a number on the kid. He slowed his pace. He was going to have to let her go for the time being. He glanced at the rear bumper of her rusty car and committed the license number to memory. He'd track down her address through the car registration and talk to her later when she'd had time to calm down.

While he watched Daisy gunned the engine, rocketing through the tall, ornate wrought-iron gates. Quinn froze with his hand on the door handle. She was going too fast to make the stop sign at the end of the short turnoff from the busy four-lane highway beyond the gate. It was rush hour;

cars and trucks and delivery vans zoomed past heedless of the small car about to enter their midst.

"Stop!" He yelled as loud as he could. Daisy must have realized the danger at almost the same moment he did and braked. The driver of a big panel van swerved to avoid her but it was too late. The right front bumper caught the sedan on the left fender and sent it spinning back across the grass, broadside, into the stone wall.

Brakes squealed and horns blared as cars swerved into the other lane to avoid the accident. Quinn started running even before the panel van had braked to a halt. The driver's side of the sedan was crumpled in on itself. There was no sign of movement from inside the car.

No sign of life.

DAISY'S HEAD WAS SPINNING from where she'd contacted the window glass. She lifted her hand to her forehead but didn't feel any blood. She groaned. The pain in her elbow and ankle almost, but not quite, overwhelmed the fear in her heart. She'd been in an accident, she knew that much, sideswiped by a big white truck that she'd never seen coming until it was too late. What had she done letting herself be panicked by her unexpected meeting with Quinn Parrish? She clasped her shaking hands around her distended middle. Was her baby all right? She fumbled for the release on her seat belt, wanting nothing more desperately than to be out of her mangled car. The air bag hadn't deployed she realized belatedly. The impact couldn't have been all that bad, right? It was just that the truck had pushed her sideways into the wall and her left side had taken the brunt of the impact.

She struggled to open the door but couldn't manage. The pain in her elbow and ankle was spreading, moving across her body, centering itself in the middle of her back, radiating into her pelvis. "Oh, no," she moaned. "No. Not yet. Not yet, little one. You're not ready to be born yet." She laid her head against the steering wheel and fought back tears.

"Daisy, are you all right?"

She lifted her head, responding to the tone of command in the voice, still a little dizzy with shock and the tightening pain in her abdomen. She found herself staring directly into Quinn Parrish's stark, white face, "Yes," she said, "no." The pain was worse, unrelenting now. This wasn't the way it was supposed to be. This isn't how they'd described how her labor would progress in the birthing classes she'd taken at the hospital.

"I'm going to get you out of here."

"Shouldn't we wait for the emergency crew?" It was another voice, a stranger's. She looked past Quinn and noticed a tall man with skin the color of coffee staring in at her with worried eyes. He was wearing a khaki shirt with his name and an auto parts company logo embroidered on the pocket. He must be the truck driver.

"Look at the way traffic's backed up," Quinn growled, wrestling the door open with both hands. "They might not be here for fifteen or twenty minutes." He hunkered down so that his line of sight was level with hers. She fixed her gaze on his face, all hard lines and angles. His expression was hard, too, but comforting all the same. He didn't look anything like Brendan, she thought distractedly, but of course he wouldn't. They weren't blood relation, just stepbrothers. He reached in the car and laid his hand on her arm. His touch was gentle. She shivered at the warmth of his touch, suddenly shaking with cold and reaction. "Daisy, are you okay? Did you hurt your back, your neck?"

"No. My elbow, and my ankle, that's all." His hand left her arm and she felt his fingers probe gently along her lower leg.

"Where does it hurt? Here?"

She winced. "Yes. That's it."

"Looks like a pretty bad sprain but I don't think it's broken. Your elbow's banged up, too. Hold tight and the ambulance will be here soon."

"I can't wait," she said, grasping his hand between her own. "I...I'm in labor. The baby's coming and it hurts so bad, way more than they said it would. I'm scared something's wrong, terribly wrong. Please, tell them to hurry." She began to cry. She couldn't seem to control herself. She had never felt so alone and helpless in her life. Pain arced through her again taking her breath away. "Please, Quinn," she said. "I need your help."

CHAPTER TWO

QUINN GLANCED AT THE waiting-room clock. Eight and a half hours since he'd looked up from his brother's gravestone and locked his gaze with Daisy Brookshire's warm, brown eyes. It seemed like a lifetime. What was taking so long? They had moved Daisy from the emergency room to the birthing center hours ago. She had been in a lot of pain even then, the bumps and bruises and sprained ankle from the accident adding to the misery of childbirth. He knew it wasn't politically correct to call labor contractions misery but it had sure looked that way to him.

He glanced across the small, cheerfully decorated room. The three women sitting side by side across from him stared back. Their expressions were friendly and polite but their body language was reserved and not one of them held his gaze for more than a moment or two. He wished he could ask them if eight hours was normal for a first baby but he had decided it was best not to show male ignorance in front of this crew. They would pounce on his weakness like lionesses at the kill.

Patsy and Juliana Grosso, and Sophia Grosso-Murphy. He had had no idea that Daisy had such powerful friends. He was looking at three generations of NASCAR royalty. Juliana Grosso's husband, Milo, old as dirt, almost the last of his breed, was still a force to be reckoned with in stock-car racing, as was his wife. Juliana was a legend in her own right. The middle-aged woman beside her was Patsy Grosso, wife of former NASCAR Sprint Cup champion, Dean Grosso, Juliana's grandson. The couple were co-owners of Cargill-Grosso Racing. Although he was more than satisfied with his association with Double S Racing he'd have given almost any amount of money to have sponsored one of Dean and Patsy's cars. Any businessman worth his corner office and expense account would. The youngest of the trio was Sophia, Patsy's daughter, and wife of NASCAR driver Justin Murphy.

He stood up and walked to the closed doors leading to the birthing suites. He hadn't been allowed in the room since Daisy's labor coach, her boss, Rue Larrabee, had shown up at the Concord hospital where Daisy had been admitted. Quinn had underestimated the efficiency of the first responders and the Concord police department. Despite the snarled traffic in both directions they had arrived in less than ten minutes and extracted Daisy from the car with quick, practiced efficiency.

He had followed the ambulance to the hospital and managed to talk the admissions people into letting him deal with the paperwork by allowing them to think he was Daisy's brother-in-law. By the time the emergency room staff was ready to transfer her to the birthing suites she'd been in too much pain to object when he followed along. He'd even stayed by her side for the first hour until Rue Larrabee arrived.

The hospital staff hadn't been a match for him but Daisy's employer was. Five feet eight inches of fiery, redheaded single-mindedness, she gave him one minute to explain who he was and what he was doing there, and then pointed a red-tipped finger at the door and told him to vamoose. She would talk to him later. Completely out of his element in the hospital setting, thrown off balance by the inner turmoil Daisy's pain had caused him, Quinn had uncharacteristically obeyed. He'd been exiled to waiting room limbo ever since.

He glanced at the clock, his mind circling back to his original unanswered questions. Was this taking too long? Was Daisy all right? Was the baby okay?

"How long have you known Daisy?" Juliana Grosso asked suddenly.

"We met for the first time today. At the cemetery," he said, roused from his musings by her demanding voice.

"You're August Carlyle's stepson, correct?" Her tone was accusatory.

"My mother is married to August Carlyle, yes," he replied carefully. His relationship with his mother's husband was practically nonexistent these days. He'd suffered August's bullying during his teenage years because he'd had no other choice but once he was out on his own he'd never set foot under the old man's roof unless his mother begged him to.

"You're Fiona Carlyle's son." Patsy's voice was softer than Juliana's but no less forceful.

"Yes, ma'am."

"We've served on several committees together. She has been a very generous donor to our family's foundation for missing and exploited children." The revelation a year before that celebrity chef Grace Clark was the long-lost daughter of Dean and Patsy Grosso had rocked NASCAR nation. He'd already made the decision that Rev Energy Drinks should sponsor a NASCAR Sprint Cup car so he had followed the drama carefully through Internet postings, even though he'd been out of the country at the time.

"My mother has many charitable interests," he said noncommittally. August Carlyle would allow nothing less from his wife.

Juliana grew impatient with their small talk. "Did you frighten poor Daisy into pulling out into traffic like that?"

"Nana," Sophia cautioned, tilting her blond head as she gave him a long, hard look that was only slightly less accusatory than her great-grandmother's.

"In some respects I am responsible," he said.

"At least you admit it."

"Why do you feel you're responsible, Mr. Parrish?" Patsy asked.

These women were Daisy's friends. It figured they would know what Brendan's father was up to and come down firmly on Daisy's side. "Finding me at Brendan's grave upset her," he said candidly. "She jumped to the conclusion that I was in agreement with my mother and August that she should give them custody of her baby after it…she…is born."

"August Carlyle is a jackass," Juliana snorted. "It's medieval what he's attempting to do to that poor girl."

Patsy laid her hand on her grandmother-in-law's arm. "Daisy is in a very difficult position financially," she reminded the older woman.

"That gives him no right to terrorize her."

"Daisy's had a rough time of it these last six months. You can understand why she doesn't want to have anything to do with your mother and stepfather," Sophia said, rising from her chair and coming toward him, her eyes searching his face as though trying to determine if he was cut from the same bolt as his stepfather and his mother. "Are you on her side or theirs?" she asked bluntly.

She held his gaze, her stance and expression nearly an exact copy of her formidable great-grandmother's. Quinn didn't make the mistake of smiling at the comparison but he wanted to. "I seldom agree with my stepfather on any matter," he replied. "I don't intend to start doing so now."

Sophia remained silent a moment or two longer, not breaking eye contact. Then she turned to her grandmother. "I believe him," she said.

Patsy nodded but Juliana opened her mouth as if to continue the argument. Quinn braced himself for another grilling but at the moment what sounded like music box chimes poured from the loudspeaker in the corner of the room, filling the air with the notes of "Rock-a-bye Baby".

"She's here," Sophia said, clapping her hands. "The nurse told us Daisy's the only mother-to-be in labor right now so it must mean that her baby's been born. Oh, I can't wait to see her."

The double doors of the birthing center swung open and Rue Larrabee sailed through. She was wearing sea-green scrubs and a surgical cap concealed her red hair but it was her blazing ear-to-ear smile that caught and held Quinn's attention. "We have our baby," she announced with a flourish. "Brianna Grace Brookshire has arrived."

CHAPTER THREE

IT WAS ALL WORTH IT, the worry about their future, the fear that she'd harmed her child when she wrecked her car, the hours of pain that had left her exhausted but exhilarated when she finally heard her baby's first cry. Daisy gazed down at the tiny, scrunched up face of her daughter and felt her heart constrict with a mixture of love and lingering sorrow. "She's beautiful, Brendan," she whispered, "so beautiful. I know you would have fallen in love with her the moment you laid eyes on her."

"I think so, too."

Daisy looked up, startled to find she wasn't alone. "Oh, it's you," she said. Quinn Parrish stood in the doorway of the birthing room, his hands in the pockets of what appeared to be a very old leather jacket. He was wearing dark gray slacks and a black T-shirt and he looked every inch the successful and ruthless businessman he was. Her heart rate had quickened in anxiety when his shadow fell across her bed. She took a deep breath to get it under control. *Remember,* her inner voice told her, *he was raised by August Carlyle. No matter what he did for you yesterday, be careful around him.* She shifted the sleeping baby in her arms, grimacing a little at the pain in her left elbow when she moved.

"Good morning," he said advancing a few steps into the room. The door was propped open. He made no move to close it and Daisy relaxed a fraction. She hadn't wanted to be alone with him, not when she was feeling so vulnerable and nearly as helpless as her infant.

"Good morning," she echoed, wondering how he had gotten into the hospital so early in the day. Visiting hours for anyone but fathers and grandparents didn't start until one o'clock in the afternoon. It was only a little after nine.

"How are you feeling?"

"I'm fine. Just stiff and sore from the accident—and the baby," she said.

"Mmm," he responded noncommittally.

Daisy felt herself flush. She looked a fright, she knew she did. Sophia had gone to her apartment the evening before to bring the small suitcase she'd packed but hadn't intended to use until after Labor Day, so she was, at least, wearing her own nightgown, a soft apple-green one, and not one of those awful hospital things that opened down the back. But beyond brushing her hair and teeth an hour or so earlier she hadn't done anything to repair the ravages of the day before.

"I'd think you'd be more than just a little stiff and sore after everything you went through yesterday." He was watching her closely, his movie star blue eyes fixed on her face with laser intensity. She wondered how many people were brave enough, or foolish enough, to try to lie to him when he looked at them like that.

"You're right. I'm a lot stiff and sore." She glanced ruefully at her left ankle encased in a soft cast, a bootlike affair that allowed her to put enough weight on it to walk back and forth to the bathroom, but nothing more.

"How long do you have to be off your feet?" he asked. His hands were still in his pockets, as though he didn't know what to do with them, she thought suddenly. She liked the idea that he might not be as completely at ease as he appeared to be. Obviously he wasn't used to being around a woman who had just given birth, or a newborn, either, for that matter. The thought gave her courage.

"I don't know. I haven't spoken to the doctor yet this morning. Not long, I hope. I…I don't want to be in here any longer than necessary." She bit her lip and dropped her gaze to Brianna's tiny pink fingers wrapped surprisingly tightly around her little finger. Her insurance was minimal. It wouldn't pay for an extended stay in the hospital. And then there were the repairs to her car to consider. She hadn't budgeted for that at all.

"Will you have help with the baby when you get home?" he asked, looking down at Brianna a little warily, reinforcing her observation that he seemed completely out of his depth around a baby.

"My mother was going to come and stay with me—my parents moved to Florida a couple of years ago—but she just got a new job. My dad's been out of work for over a year, Mom almost as long."

"You haven't even told them the baby's here, have you?" he asked astutely.

She tensed and Brianna screwed up her tiny red face and frowned as though she sensed Daisy's uneasiness with his uncanny ability to almost read her mind. She shook her head. "I know she'll want to fly right up here and stay to help me. I can't ask her to do that when jobs are so hard to find." Now, why had she told him that? Shown him another vulnerability; the fact that her parents wouldn't be able to help her and the baby financially. It was another weapon August Carlyle could use against her if he found out. She felt tears burn behind her eyes and hurriedly blinked the weakness away.

"You won't be able to take care of the baby alone," he said, stating the obvious, "not for a few days at least."

"I'll be fine," she said stubbornly. "I have friends. They'll help me."

"I'm sure they will but you'll need to stay off your feet for at least a week. I'm not an obstetrician but you don't have to be a doctor to know you can't carry an infant around when you're using crutches and have a bum elbow, too."

He was right. What should she do? She wished Rue or her friend, Mellie Donovan, or Sophia were here. They would help her figure something out. If only her little apartment wasn't a third-floor walk-up, then she wouldn't worry so much, but it was and there was nowhere else for her to go when she was released from the hospital.

"I think you should come home with me."

"What?" She couldn't do that. Remember who he is, her inner voice warned. "No, that's impossible," she blurted out before she could stop herself. Brianna began to frown harder in her sleep. Her tiny hand fumbled its way to her mouth. She began to suck her thumb. Daisy wanted nothing more than to watch this remarkable action take place but she kept her eyes firmly on Quinn Parrish's hard, handsome face.

"Why?" he asked reasonably.

"I...I barely know you," she said, lifting Brianna to her shoulder, patting her back with agitated little taps, more soothing to her than to the baby.

"We're family."

His mother had been Brendan's stepmother, that hardly made them family. She opened her mouth to refute that dubious claim but shut it again with a snap. Fiona and August Carlyle stood in the doorway of her room. How had they found out Brianna had been born? She had been adamant that no information about her be given out by the hospital staff. She turned accusing eyes on Quinn Parrish. He met her angry stare head-on and gave a little shake of his head.

"It wasn't me, Daisy," he said so softly only she could hear. "Believe me, I never said a word."

"QUINN, WHAT ARE YOU DOING here?" There was genuine surprise in his mother's voice as her eyes met his across Daisy's bed. Behind her August Carlyle frowned, his thin lips tightening into a disapproving and suspicious line. The hard look didn't faze Quinn—he was used to it.

"Hello, Mom. August," he said.

"Answer your mother. What are you doing here?" August demanded, his tone clipped and as disapproving as his stare. Three hundred years of breeding and money had given him an aura of aristocratic hauteur that always grated on Quinn's nerves.

"I met Daisy by chance at the cemetery yesterday," Quinn explained. "Luckily I was close by when she had her accident. I stopped by this morning to see how she and the baby are doing."

"That's why we're here, too. Hello, Daisy." His mother looked fabulous, just as she always did. Her silver-gray hair was styled to perfection, her manicure was flawless, her clothes designer, but he could see signs of strain around her eyes and the corners of her mouth beneath her expertly applied makeup.

"How did you know I was here?" Daisy demanded, ignoring the pleasantries just as August had. Quinn silently approved of her tactics.

"The police report of your accident said you'd been brought here. We...we didn't know about the baby until we asked for you at the main desk." Fiona's explanation was too pat, too rehearsed sounding. His mother had never been a good liar. Quinn suspected August had been keeping Daisy under surveillance, probably ever since his brother had died.

"You've been spying on me." Daisy continued patting the little one on the back but her movements were more agitated and the baby squirmed against her shoulder.

"May we come in?"

"I guess so since you're already here." Quinn could see the tension in Daisy's neck and shoulders beneath the pale green cotton of her nightgown. He stayed where he was beside her bed. She slid him a quick glance from the corner of her eye but continued to focus her attention on the older couple.

Fiona advanced to within a couple of feet of the bed, drawn to the baby as though the tiny being was reeling her in by the heartstrings. His mother had raised Brendan from the time he was four years old. She had loved him deeply. Emotionally she would consider Daisy's baby her grandchild. Quinn felt a quick stab of remorse. His mother was hurting and he had done little if anything to help lessen her pain.

Fiona noticed the cast on Daisy's ankle. "Is it broken?" she asked.

"Just sprained, that's all." Daisy spoke warily.

"I'm so glad you are both all right." She clasped her hands in front of her as though she was having trouble restraining herself from reaching out to touch Daisy's baby. "I really am."

"I know," Daisy said, her voice softening slightly as her eyes met his mother's. If there was any chance of reconciling Daisy and his parents it would have to come through Fiona's efforts, Quinn knew. But in twenty years of marriage he couldn't recall a single instance where she had gone against her autocratic and demanding husband's wishes.

"How long do you have to wear that thing?" August said, indicating the cast with a flick of his index finger.

"A...a couple of weeks."

"How do you expect to take care of an infant on your own?"

"I'll manage." Her voice didn't waver. "I don't want any help from you."

"You might not have a choice, girl. If you're not able to take care of my grandchild properly then it's my duty to alert the authorities, have the child removed to a safer environment."

"No." Daisy's cry came from her heart.

"August," his mother's voice was soft but surprisingly firm. "What my husband means is that we would like you to come home with us. We have lots of room. We have spoken to a woman with excellent child care references to be…what did you name her?" she asked, unable to contain her curiosity any longer.

"Brianna. Brianna Grace."

"What a lovely name. How much does she weigh? How long is she?" It seemed that once she'd started asking questions about the baby she couldn't stop.

"She's twenty inches long and she weighs six pounds and three ounces." Rue Larrabee had told Quinn those were good numbers for a baby who had arrived two weeks earlier than expected.

"Quinn weighed over eight pounds and his head was as big as a basketball—"

"Fiona," August said reprovingly.

"I'm sorry, I'm rambling, aren't I."

Quinn felt his hands curl into fists. He hated it when his stepfather belittled her in public that way.

"Please, excuse me."

"Thank you for the offer, Mrs. Carlyle," Daisy said with dignity. "But I'm not leaving here with you, nor do I intend to be beholden to you in any way."

"No matter how my wife is trying to sugarcoat the matter, I meant what I said," August interrupted with his usual lack of tact. "If you aren't physically able to care for the child I'll be forced to intercede with the authorities—"

"That won't be necessary," Quinn said, unable to remain silent while his stepfather bullied Daisy the way he bullied everyone else. "Because she's moving in with me until her ankle is healed."

CHAPTER FOUR

"OH HONEY, ARE YOU SURE you want to do this?"

Rue was standing by the bassinet watching Brianna as she slept. Daisy had already dressed the baby in an adorable little pink and white outfit that Sophia and Patsy had dropped off an hour earlier.

"I don't have a choice really." Daisy was sitting in a chair by the window of her room. The view of the parking lot wasn't inspiring but it looked like it was going to be a nice day. She, too, was dressed to go home in drawstring slacks and a loose-fitting top, although both of them were now too large to be truly comfortable anymore. She glanced out the big window. "I can't climb the stairs to my apartment," she explained to her volatile employer. "I won't go to Brendan's parents' house." She shuddered. "I can't."

"Don't think about them," Rue commanded, reaching down to stroke Brianna's cheek as she lay in the clear-sided bassinet—sucking her thumb. She had been doing that the day Daisy had had her ultrasound and learned the baby's sex. The technician had chuckled and said, "You'll have your work cut out for you in a year or two breaking the habit." Daisy wasn't worried about that just yet; right now she thought everything her daughter did was adorable.

"You should come and stay with me, Lord knows there's plenty of room in Andrew's house," Rue insisted.

"No, I can't do that, either." Daisy longed for a moment to say yes but Rue and Andrew Clark, Patsy Grosso's brother, had just moved in together themselves and she would feel even more uncomfortable as a fifth wheel in Andrew's big house than she would in Quinn Parrish's.

"Don't be silly," Rue protested. "You shouldn't be alone."

"I'm not. I'm trying to be practical and levelheaded." The kind of traits she would need to cultivate as a single mother.

"You barely know the man."

There was no arguing with that statement. But she knew some things about him: that he had loved his brother, that he wouldn't be bullied by August Carlyle, but it infuriated him when his mother allowed herself to be diminished by that terrible man, and that like most men, babies made him nervous. For now those glimpses of his character and personality would have to be enough.

"Patsy and Sophia are both okay with this. They know him better than I do. Patsy and Dean know everyone in NASCAR. He's not a stranger to them," she reminded her employer patiently—another quality she would need in abundance, she suspected.

"Well, I suppose I can't argue with that endorsement," Rue said but she didn't sound convinced, even if Patsy Grosso would be her sister-in-law at some point in the not too distant future. "But if he gives you any grief at all pick up the phone and give me a call, you hear?"

"Thanks, Rue." A nurse appeared in the doorway with what appeared to be a small cooler and a handful of pamphlets.

"Here's Brianna's formula and the information I promised you on the baby's vaccinations and schedules for her doctor's visits, and yours," she said. "Be sure to put the formula in the fridge as soon as you get home."

"Thank you," Daisy said. She had wanted so badly to nurse Brianna but the necessity of returning to work at Cut

'N' Chat as soon as possible meant it would be more manageable to bottle feed her daughter. The nursing coach had been sympathetic but Daisy was still torn by her decision.

"Any more questions?" the plump middle-aged nurse asked, smiling down at Brianna as she automatically checked the baby's wrist bracelet against the matching one Daisy wore.

"Not that I can think of." Daisy was torn between wanting to get out of the expensive hospital room and her reluctance to face Quinn Parrish once more.

"If you do have any questions or problems you have our hotline number on every pamphlet. Remember we're here 24/7/365. Babies are what we do."

"I won't forget." Daisy smiled in spite of her inner turmoil. The hospital staff had been great.

"Push your call button when you're ready to leave. I'll take you down to the lobby."

"Thanks."

The nurse tucked a corner of Brianna's blanket more snugly around her feet and sailed out of the room.

"You're sure this is what you want to do?" Rue asked one more time when they were alone again.

"I'm sure."

"Then I'd better be getting back to the shop."

"You should have left half an hour ago." It was a long drive back to Mooresville. Rue was taking all of Daisy's appointments as well as her own longtime patrons. She would be swamped the rest of the day. Anxiety tightened her nerves, allowing the fears and worries she'd done her best to suppress to vault to the forefront of her thoughts again.

"I have plenty of time," Rue insisted. "Remember I was doing hair before you were out of diapers. I can handle twice as many bookings as we have today if I wanted to." She flexed a well-toned arm in a Rosy-the-Riveter pose. Daisy knew about Rosy-the-Riveter because there was a poster of the World War II icon in the back room of Cut 'N' Chat where Rue's male customers preferred to get their hair cut.

"I believe you," Daisy replied with a laugh. Her smile faded away, however, when she looked up and saw Quinn Parrish standing in the doorway of her room. He wasn't wearing the leather bomber jacket today, but even in rolled up shirtsleeves and a subdued gray power tie he looked more handsome and sexy than any mortal man had a right to be. Sexy? Where had that come from? She wasn't used to thinking of men in those terms anymore. Must be the upheaval in her hormone levels, she decided, and did her best to put the unsettling image out of her mind.

She had the feeling it might be easier said than done.

SHE WAS SITTING IN A HIGH-back chair near the window, dressed in dark gray slacks and a lightweight cotton top the color of a ripe strawberry. Her hair was pulled back from her face with two sparkly clips and a pair of gold hoops dangled from her ears. She had nice ears, Quinn noticed for the first time, small and close to her head. She had a nice nose, too, just a little snub with a smattering of freckles across the bridge. There was color in her cheeks and a smile on her face. She looked closer to sixteen than twenty-five.

"Hello, Daisy. Ms. Larrabee," he said.

Daisy looked across the room at him and her smile faltered for a moment, then returned in a more subdued way. "Hello, Quinn."

"Might as well call me Rue," her friend said, nodding in his direction, "seeing as how Daisy's going home with you."

"Thanks, Rue. I'll take good care of her, I promise."

"You'd better," the older woman instructed, "or you'll have me to answer to."

She picked up a huge shoulder bag that looked as if it

could hold a month's supply of groceries and stooped to give Daisy a hug. "Call me when you're settled in."

"I will."

She gave Quinn one more look that told him she still wasn't sure she trusted him so he'd better watch his step and left the room.

"She means well," Daisy said. He turned his head and found her watching him. Had he let his thoughts show that clearly? He didn't ordinarily do that. In fact he never did that.

"You've got loyal friends," he said.

"They've been great to me." Her eyes filled with tears. She dashed them away with an impatient hand. "Hormones," she said. "They warned me this would happen."

He didn't like to see her cry. It made him want to take her in his arms and hold her close, soothe her, protect her. *Whoa! Wait a minute.* He steered clear of needy women. They reminded him too forcefully of his mother when he was a little boy, scared and alone, a single mother working two jobs to keep him in sneakers and feed him frozen pizzas. So desperate to latch on to the security that August Carlyle offered that she lived under his thumb to this very day. "No problem," he said. "I saw the nurse at the desk. She's getting a wheelchair for you. Do you have everything ready to go?"

She motioned to the small suitcase and a soft-sided cooler on the bed. He wondered what was in the cooler. He spotted an empty formula bottle on the bedside table and came up with an educated guess. She wasn't breast-feeding the baby, it seemed.

Was it a personal choice, or because she was going to have to go back to work as soon as she could? He had no right to ask about such a personal decision and he didn't intend to. He hadn't considered the physical intimacy having Daisy living with him would entail but it was too late to worry about that now.

And then there was the baby.

From time to time he'd speculated on what it would be like living with a woman but putting a baby into the scenario had never entered his thoughts before today.

Quinn glanced at the sleeping infant in the plastic bassinet. Babies were small, fragile and easily breakable. He'd never handled one in his life. Daisy was still on crutches. Why hadn't he taken that into consideration sooner than this very moment? He'd thought far enough ahead to buy a top-of-the-line car seat and a small crib and changing table to put in the bedroom of his century-old cabin but that was all. He hadn't made arrangements for a nurse or a nanny even though he had a reputation for long-range planning that usually met any contingency. Too late he saw his mistake. It was inevitable he would have to pick Brianna up sooner or later. Maybe even change her diaper. The image boggled his mind.

What the heck had he gotten himself into?

CHAPTER FIVE

"HERE WE ARE."

Daisy woke from a half doze and looked out the window of the big SUV. Blinked and then blinked again. She had assumed that Quinn Parrish lived the same lifestyle as his mother and stepfather, a palatial home in a secluded, gated community where all the women were thin and tanned and toned and all the men were successful and powerful beyond her wildest dreams. Brendan had taken her to his parents' home once—all stone and brick and huge arched windows— when the older couple was in Europe. She had seen how the other half lived.

Quinn's home was a weathered log cabin with a steeply pitched roof and a river-rock fireplace, nestled in a small clearing surrounded by pine trees at the end of a gravel lane. They had left Concord behind them and climbed into the low rolling hills above Lake Norman, but even though the lake wasn't visible through the trees, Daisy suspected they weren't all that far from golf courses and marinas and the homes of NASCAR's most successful drivers and owners.

Quinn's cabin looked as if it had come from another time, another place. A covered porch stretched across the front and along one side. Big old hickory rocking chairs sat on either side of a small wicker table. To the left of the house a dilapidated barn, with weathered siding and missing shingles on its roof, listed slightly to one side, as though leaning into the wind that danced through the top of the pine trees. The yard was overgrown with wildflowers, an ancient rosebush had climbed up one of the porch railings and halfway across the roof a few blood-red blooms, protected from the late summer heat, peeked out here and there among the leaves.

"It's not what you expected, is it?" Quinn asked, his hands resting on the steering wheel.

"No," she said before she could stop herself. "It's not." The grass needed cutting, the trim on the porch and windows needed a coat of paint and the rosebush was in desperate need of pruning, but the cabin itself looked strong and sturdy and…welcoming. She hadn't expected that, either.

"This land has been in my family for a hundred years. My great-grandfather built this cabin after he came home from World War I. My father grew up here."

"Is your father still living?" She knew so little about this man.

"He died when I was three. A motorcycle accident. He was going too fast down a dirt road by the lake, lost control and slammed into a tree. He died instantly. Except for a couple of cousins out in California I'm the last of my family."

"I'm sorry," she said. Family was important to her, even though hers was far away. Sophia had e-mailed photos of her holding Brianna to her parents. After much reassurance that Daisy was okay, they decided they wouldn't be able to make the trip to see their new grandbaby for at least a month. She felt like crying again but didn't give in to the urge.

"So am I," Quinn replied as he unfastened his seat belt. "Everyone should have a family to rely on."

Daisy missed his last remark; her attention was focused elsewhere. Another problem had revealed itself. She wasn't looking forward to maneuvering across the rutted driveway and up the steps into the cabin on crutches. Quinn appeared beside her open door. "You first and then the baby," he said in his calm, authoritative way.

"I'm planning my route," she said.

"I have a better idea." He reached down, unsnapped her seat belt. "I'll carry you."

"There's no need for that. I can walk," she insisted, mortified.

"I don't want you to do any more damage to your ankle putting your foot in a rabbit hole. This yard's a minefield."

He was right—the yard was a minefield of trailing weeds and rabbit holes; she couldn't deny that so she stopped protesting. He slid his arm beneath her knees and lifted her effortlessly into his arms. Instinctively she looped her arm around his neck. She could feel the strength in his back and shoulders as he turned with her held high against his chest. He might spend most of his time seated behind a desk but he was in no way soft. He was all man, from the stubble of afternoon beard that darkened his chin to the subtle expensive scent of his aftershave and soap, and the ripple of solid muscle beneath the soft Egyptian cotton of his shirt. They crossed the small yard and climbed the steps to the porch. He set her down in one of the old rocking chairs that creaked obligingly as she settled into it. She couldn't seem to take her eyes off him and watched as he strode back to the SUV to unfasten Brianna from the car seat he'd arrived at the hospital with.

Daisy had no idea how she was going to pay him for the top-of-the-line baby carrier. She didn't like to be beholden to anyone but there was no way the hospital would let her take Brianna away without one, and she hadn't had a chance to buy one at the consignment shop where'd she'd been picking up twice-but-nice baby clothes for the last couple of months.

In the best tradition of Scarlett O'Hara she would worry about her mounting debt to Quinn Parrish another day. For now all she wanted was a chance to hold her baby again. Brianna had started fussing a little a couple of miles from the cabin, sucking her tiny fist, making faint mewing sounds just like a kitten. She was hungry. It seemed she was always hungry, already taking three ounces of formula every three hours.

Quinn returned to the porch, Brianna's carrier in one hand, Daisy's crutches in the other. Evidently he hadn't been any more comfortable carrying her in his arms than she had been being carried. He handed her the crutches. "I'll hold the door," he said, suiting action to words. Brianna was fussing louder now, the tiny kitten cries growing into full-fledged howls of impatience and hunger. Quinn glanced down at the infant with a frown that seemed more puzzled than annoyed. "Wow," he said, holding the old-fashioned wooden screen door open for Daisy to precede him into the cabin. "She's not a happy camper."

"She's hungry," Daisy apologized. "She'll be quiet again as soon as I feed her." What if she was misreading his quizzical expression? What if he was truly annoyed? What if he didn't like having a baby around? What would he do if Brianna got a tummy ache and wouldn't stop crying? Daisy felt a little frisson of fear slither up and down her nerve endings. After all, she really didn't know anything about this man. He could be a monster in disguise, even if the Grosso women and even Rue had all given their okay for her to spend the next two weeks in his hilltop hideaway. Her thoughts kept spinning around in her brain and her head was beginning to ache as badly as her ankle.

Quinn opened the door and stepped back, waiting for her to enter first. "Oh!" Daisy stepped across the threshold and caught her breath in surprise, immediately ashamed of her earlier wild-eyed imaginings. This wasn't some playboy hideaway. In fact it was almost the opposite of what you would expect of a man of Quinn Parrish's wealth and importance: mismatched tables and lamps, threadbare carpet, limp and faded chintz drapes at the windows, the entire space dominated by a smoke-darkened fireplace that took up most of the wall on her right-hand side. Nothing here was new, or shiny or terribly expensive.

Except for the items she spotted in the middle of the room. There was a white wicker bassinette with pink lace lining, a matching changing table, stacks of cloth diapers, packages of disposable ones, boxes filled with bottles, cases of formula, a bottle warmer, baby wipes, what appeared to be an entire layette in shades of pink and apple-green and sunny yellow, tiny fleece blankets and a big, fluffy white stuffed puppy sitting on the couch, keeping watch over it all.

Daisy sucked in her breath. All the things she needed for the baby, all the things she wanted and couldn't afford. Quinn, a man she barely knew, had bought them for her. The enormity of the debt she owed Brendan's brother threatened to overwhelm her.

The screen door slapped shut behind her. She swiveled awkwardly on the crutches to find Quinn with the quilted diaper bag her friends Mellie Donovan and Sheila True-blood, from Maudie's Down Home Diner, had brought to the hospital the day before, slung over his shoulder and her now-squalling daughter in her carrier in the other hand. She was so tired and sore and at the same time she felt, absurdly, that she'd come home. "You shouldn't have," she whispered. "You just shouldn't have." She limped to the worn leather chair set at a right angle to an equally worn sofa, dropped onto the seat, buried her face in her hands and burst into tears.

CHAPTER SIX

QUINN LOOKED UP from his computer screen and laced his hands behind his head as he swiveled his desk chair to look out the window. He'd just gotten off the phone with Gil Sizemore. The topic of their discussion, as usual, was Gil's driver Eli Ward. A few days before the night race at Bristol Quinn had laid down the law to the charismatic, but erratic, NASCAR Sprint Cup driver threatening to withdraw his sponsorship if Eli didn't rein in his high-flying lifestyle and begin driving up to his potential.

The shock of losing a twelve million dollar sponsorship seemed to have done the trick and Eli finished sixth at the famed Tennessee short track. Not that Quinn wanted to withdraw his sponsorship of the No. 502 car, but he would if he had to. He wasn't paying that kind of money to sponsor the playboy of the Western world. He wanted to see the Rev Energy Drinks car in Victory Lane as badly as Gil Sizemore and his team did. Quinn crossed his legs on the scarred windowsill and looked past his shoes to the neglected yard. Eli was a natural, a born race-car driver, a born showman. His rivalry with Double S Racing's top dog, Rafael O'Bryan, had been worth its weight in gold as far as publicity and product placement went. But having an out of control driver associated with Rev Energy Drinks wasn't the image Quinn wanted to project. He sighed. Time would tell.

He continued to stare out into the backyard. It was even more neglected than the front of the house—if that was possible. The lingering summer twilight had smudged the stark outline of the old barn and softened the ragged edges of the overgrown vegetable garden he remembered his grandmother tending when he was a little boy. The soft light hid a lot of the blemishes, making it all appear a little more as he remembered it from his childhood, before his mother married August Carlyle and took him away from the one place he'd ever felt like calling home.

He picked up his glass of whiskey and took a swallow letting the smooth liquor slide down the back of his throat. He hadn't been able to spend much time out here in the decade since his grandparents had died within three months of each other, his grandfather from a heart attack, his grandmother from a broken heart, he suspected. But since he'd returned to the States it had become his base of operations. He settled lower in his chair, rubbing the back of his neck to relieve the ache of sitting too long hunched over a computer screen. He wondered if his grandparents had had any inkling how much their hardscrabble farm would be worth one day. Probably a pretty good one or they wouldn't have held on to it through good times and bad, watching the march of progress along the shore of Lake Norman grow closer with each passing year.

He'd mortgaged the farm to the hilt to enter into partnership with an old college friend whose equally hardworking ancestors had left him a small, marginally profitable soft drink bottling company. Together they developed Rev Energy Drinks. His partner had been the brains; he'd been the marketing talent. Rev had taken off just as they hoped it would—a genuine overnight success—if you counted five years of eighty-hour workweeks an overnight success. Rev Energy Drinks had found its niche market in the newest generation of NASCAR nation and since then they hadn't looked back.

And best of all he'd done it without taking one red cent from August Carlyle.

A sound caught Quinn's attention and overrode his memories with more immediate concerns. Daisy was up and moving around in his bedroom—he'd been sleeping on a futon in his office since she'd been staying at the cabin. He'd had the plumbing and electrical circuits upgraded, put in central air and a new furnace and bought a flat screen TV for the living room but beyond that the place was pretty much the same as it had been when his grandparents lived here, including slippery pine floors and what seemed like dozens and dozens of throw rugs—dangerous for a woman on crutches, especially one who had given birth to a baby only a few days ago.

He surged out of his chair and headed down the short, dark hallway toward the main room. Sure enough Daisy was up and headed down the hallway. She was still wearing the clothes she'd left the hospital in but she'd pulled her hair up into a kind of swirly knot on top of her head. The effect of the hairstyle made her look closer to her true age than she had that afternoon, but she still seemed very young to be a mother. There were dark circles of fatigue shadowing her huge, brown eyes and he was reminded yet again of all she'd gone through in the last seventy-two hours. He wondered if she should even be out of bed.

"What do you need? What can I get for you?"

She gestured toward the bathroom doorway, her face turning pink. "Oh," he said, hastily. "I...I guess I can't—"

"Right," she said. "I'll have to manage the bathroom on my own."

"Um, sure." He ran his hand through his hair. He had lived alone for so long it threw him off stride to have someone sharing his space, especially a woman.

And a baby.

As though the thought was her cue, Brianna began to

fuss and then cry. Quinn glanced at his watch. Exactly three hours since Daisy had fed her after he'd settled them and all their paraphernalia in his bedroom. That had been a disaster, too. He hadn't known what to do when she started crying—Daisy, not the baby.

He'd never considered the fact that she would feel she had to reimburse him for all those things; he'd only wanted Brendan's baby to have whatever she needed so he'd had his middle-aged, motherly personal assistant buy them for him and have them delivered to the cabin. He'd had to do some fast thinking and fast talking to persuade Daisy she didn't have to pay him a cent. If she really wanted to buy her own things for Brianna after she left his care, he'd told her, then he would donate all these things to a women's shelter. She had agreed to go along with that plan, but reluctantly. She was adamant she didn't want to be any more in his debt—in his family's debt—than she already was.

It had taken all Quinn's considerable willpower not to prolong the argument by insisting that he in no way considered himself a part of August Carlyle's family, no matter how much he had loved his charming, heedless and self-indulgent stepbrother. He had thrown out the donation to the women's shelter as a way to end the standoff and Daisy had stopped crying.

He wished he could say the same for her daughter. He could hear water running in the bathroom. He wondered how long Daisy would be in there. Should he tap on the door and tell her Brianna needed her?

Or should he go get the baby himself?

Brianna began crying harder and louder. The water was still running. The trembling, infant howls were impossible to ignore. He walked into his bedroom and stared down at the tiny being in the bassinette. Her face was red and her eyes were squeezed shut. He wondered what color they were. Blue, he supposed. Most babies had blue eyes when they were born, didn't they? But he'd never seen her awake in the hospital so he couldn't be certain.

She must have sensed someone was in the room with her because for a moment she stopped crying, opened her eyes—he still couldn't tell what color they were in the dim light—and stared up at him for the space of a couple of heartbeats. She didn't look like Brendan. She didn't even look like Daisy that he could see. She just looked...like a baby. Then she smiled, or did something with her mouth that looked like a smile—and his heart flipped over in his chest.

She was beautiful, even red-faced and wrinkly.

She'd howled again and kicked off all her blankets. Once her legs were free they began to pump in spasmodic jerks. One of her little booties had come off and he marveled for a moment at her perfect baby-doll-size feet. Maybe she was cold? He reached out and touched her miniature toes with the tip of his finger. They were velvet soft and cool to the touch. He picked up the little pink bootie and slipped it back on, then tucked the blankets around her as best he could. She stopped crying and stared fixedly at him, or at least she seemed to be staring at him. He'd read somewhere that newborns couldn't see objects that weren't very close to them.

Evidently his face was close enough because she was definitely staring at him. Quinn straightened up slowly and prepared to tiptoe out of the room. Her tiny fists flailed in the air and she started crying again. He didn't know what to do to make her stop. Chilly toes obviously weren't her only problem. She wanted to be fed, or changed, or something else he couldn't decipher. He needed to get Daisy out of the bathroom to tend to her; he certainly couldn't do it. Could he?

Maybe he could. How hard could it be to pick up a baby

barely heavier than a sack of sugar, and hold her until her mother could take her?

Really hard, he decided and turned on his heel, determined to stand outside the bathroom and pound on the door until Daisy answered.

He didn't have to. Daisy was standing in the doorway, balanced on her crutches, watching him with her daughter. He wondered briefly how long she'd been there. Long enough to have seen him touch the baby?

He cleared his throat. "She's cold, I think," he said.

"And hungry," Daisy added, tilting her head to give him a Madonna-like half smile. "I'll fix her a bottle."

"No, I'll do it."

She looked as if she would refuse his help, then must have decided better of it. "Thank you," she said, the smile fading away to a slightly anxious look. "I don't know my way around your kitchen yet. It will be quicker if you do it. Not too warm, you know, just so it feels comfortable on the inside of your wrist."

He'd seen people do that on TV. He could handle that. He nodded.

"If you hand her to me I'll feed her here." She pointed to the rocker his grandmother had kept in the kitchen, the room with the biggest windows, where she could sit and rock and watch over her half dozen birdfeeders made from gourds she grew in the garden. His bedroom wasn't as bright or cheerful as the kitchen. The single window was small and high up on the wall. The room looked gloomy and dark, and face it, downright shabby, something he hadn't really paid much attention to before this very moment.

"Would you be more comfortable in the living room?" he asked.

Daisy's expression brightened momentarily. "I...I don't want to disturb your evening," she said, not quite meeting his eyes straight on.

"You're not disturbing me. I was just going to watch an old John Wayne movie on TV. Want to join me?"

"I love John Wayne movies." Daisy's smile was spontaneous and bright as sunlight. She laughed and it sounded like the tinkling glass of the old-fashioned wind chimes that still hung beside the back door.

"Great. Make yourself comfortable in the living room and I'll get Brianna's bottle ready."

"Will you carry her for me?"

That stopped him cold. "Carry her?" He hadn't had to deal with picking up the baby—until now.

"I can't manage with the crutches," she said, giving him a quizzical look. "You do know how to pick up a baby, don't you?"

"Well, I uh—"

"You've never held a baby?" She sounded as if she couldn't quite believe her own ears.

"I was an only child," he explained and knew it wasn't much of an excuse.

"Well," she said with a mischievous sparkle in her brown eyes. "You're going to have to learn. Ready?"

"Ready," he said, not sure he was at all.

"Put one hand under her head and one hand under her bottom and lift."

"That's it?"

"That's it. Oh, and don't drop her. Babies are champion wigglers."

"Gotcha."

"Think you can manage?"

"I was a wide receiver in high school. I'm pretty good at holding on to a football. She's not a whole lot bigger than a football." He hoped he sounded confident because he wasn't. He reached down and did as Daisy had instructed. The moment he slipped his hands beneath Brianna's head and little bottom she stopped crying. She felt light as a feather in his hands. He propped her against his shoulder being careful to keep his hand at the back of her neck so her head didn't flop around, the way he'd seen other men do when they were holding an infant.

He turned his head to see Daisy staring at him with a strange, sad look on her face. "What's wrong?" he asked, and then answered his own question. "You're thinking it should be my stepbrother holding the baby."

She blinked; her eyes bright with unshed tears. "Yes," she said, "I was thinking of Brendan. But not for the reason you're thinking. Not because I still love him, but only because Brianna will never know him and that is so very sad."

"We'll tell her about him. We'll show her pictures," Quinn said, jiggling the baby very gently against his shoulder, not because he'd seen someone else do it, but because it seemed the right thing to do. "We'll watch all the videos of his birthdays and Little League games. My mom has hours and hours of them." It was the wrong thing to say; he knew it the moment the words left his mouth.

"Sure. Someday." Daisy's expression turned guarded and she refused to meet his gaze once more. "Maybe I'll just feed her in here, after all."

"No," Quinn said, "go on into the living room. We won't mention my mother or my stepfather again."

"I'm sorry," she said, turning awkwardly on the crutches. She looked back at him over her shoulder. "It's just—"

"My mother raised Brendan from the time he was four," he explained, owing his mother that much loyalty at least. "She loved him like a son."

"I can't help the way I feel right now," Daisy said. She looked as if she might start crying again.

"You don't have to explain. I promised you in the hospital they wouldn't bother you here. I gave you my word. I'll stand by it."

"Thank you." She began to limp toward the living room. "But I won't put you in the middle again. I'll fight my own battles with your parents when the time comes."

CHAPTER SEVEN

"I CAN'T BELIEVE BRIANNA'S ten days old already," Mellie Donovan whispered, smiling down at the baby in her carrier. Mellie was a couple of years younger than Daisy, raising a toddler, Lily, on her own. Sheila had introduced the two of them one day not long after Mellie started waiting tables at Maudie's Down Home Diner and they had become friends. They were sitting on the porch of Quinn's cabin in the big, old hickory rockers watching as Lily squatted in front of Brianna's carrier, inspecting the fascinating live doll baby that Daisy had produced from her big fat belly. It was early evening, warm and muggy with a hint of thunder in the air, typical Labor Day weekend weather in North Carolina.

"I can't believe how quickly the days have gone by," Daisy marveled. She'd slept away most of the first few days she'd been at Quinn's cabin, surfacing only long enough to feed Brianna and then tumbling back down onto her bed or curling up on the couch to nap with her daughter cuddled in her arms.

Quinn had been true to his word. He hadn't allowed his mother and stepfather to even speak to her on the phone, let alone show up on his doorstep. But everyone else she knew had no problem getting past her vigilant host. She'd been visited by all her friends, and several of the Tuesday Tarts, the group of mostly NASCAR wives and mothers and team members—and even female drivers like Kelsey Kendall—

who met in a back room of Maudie's each week for food and fellowship—and good-natured gossip.

Someone had made the trip out from Mooresville every day, bearing gifts and hampers of food, "oohing" and "ahhing" over her daughter, and she suspected, checking to see if she was getting along okay with Brendan's formidable stepbrother. The answer was she was surprisingly comfortable living with a man she barely knew, something she hadn't expected would be the case.

Quinn would be pleased to see the thick slices of meat loaf, mashed potatoes, country gravy and homemade pecan pie from Maudie's Sheila had unloaded into the old-fashioned round-shouldered refrigerator in the kitchen. He knew his way around a can opener and microwave but he confessed that was about the extent of his cooking expertise. Happily he hadn't had to do much cooking. Even Juliana Grosso had made the journey from her home to their hilltop retreat bearing a savings bond to seed Brianna's college fund, and a casserole of her world famous lasagna. They'd just finished the last of it the evening before. Daisy had begun to despair of ever losing the extra five pounds she still needed to get rid of to get back into her favorite clothes.

Sheila stuck her head out the door and sucked in her breath. "It's too hot to eat out here. Let's have an indoor picnic instead," she said in her customary take-charge tone. "Come inside, everything's ready."

Daisy levered herself to her feet, using the arms of the rocker. She'd abandoned the crutches the day before in favor of an ankle brace and she was getting around pretty well in the house. She still let someone else carry Brianna, usually Quinn, but her elbow was healing even more quickly than her ankle, so she was no longer afraid it would give out on her and she would drop her daughter on her head.

"The mosquitoes are ferocious already and it's barely

noon," Mellie complained. "We don't want Brianna bitten to pieces."

"Don't like sqeeter bites," Lily seconded, giving her arm a slap. Lily had curly brown hair and brown eyes, chubby cheeks and a heart-melting smile.

Inside Sheila had set out plates and napkins and dishes of made-from-scratch salads and fresh bread and fluffy key lime tartlets on the low pine table in front of the sofa. "Mmm," Lily said, delighted that all the food was on her level. She plopped down on a throw pillow on the floor and rested her elbows on the table. "I'm hungry. Let's eat."

"I agree." Daisy laughed. Everything looked so good she could hardly wait to begin.

"There's a NASCAR retrospective on TV that I'd like to see," Sheila explained. "Do you suppose Quinn will mind if I turn on that gigantic flat screen?" It was a measure of how off-balance Daisy had been when she arrived at the cabin that it had taken her several hours to notice the huge TV hidden in the shadows above the fireplace mantel.

"Of course he won't mind. The remote's on the table by your chair."

Sheila studied the remote for a moment then pressed the power button. "I can't get used to having all these famous and almost famous people hanging around Maudie's. I need to bone-up on my racing history so I don't make a fool of myself—"

"Around Gil Sizemore, you mean?" Mellie interrupted, giving Daisy an exaggerated wink that she knew perfectly well Sheila would intercept.

"What's this?" Daisy asked, sitting down on the couch while Mellie deposited Brianna's carrier at her feet. "Gil Sizemore? The owner of Double S Racing?" She'd seen pictures of the handsome team owner on some of the glossy advertising copy Quinn had scattered around the cabin.

"He's becoming quite the regular at Maudie's these days.

He says it's the meat loaf sandwiches. He can't get enough of them." Mellie dropped down cross-legged beside Lily, helping her to a peanut butter and jelly sandwich with the crust cut off the bread that Sheila had obviously made especially for the little girl. "Personally I don't think it's the meat loaf that keeps him coming back, but Sheila won't give him the time of day."

"Gil isn't sitting at my front counter any more often than Bart Branch," Sheila fired back, frowning down at her young friend. "Double S Racing's garage is barely a mile from the diner. Where else would he go to get a good home-cooked meal?"

"I'm sure that's the only reason either of those two ever step foot inside Maudie's," Daisy said, feigning innocence as she reached for a slice of ham and a big scoop of potato salad. She just hoped Brianna stayed asleep for another fifteen minutes so she could enjoy her meal and the time with her friends catching up on the gossip from Maudie's and the Tarts. She'd suspected for some time that Mellie might be harboring more-than-just-friends feelings for Bart Branch, but it was news to her that Sheila might have the same kind of interest in Gil Sizemore.

She'd never met the man. He traveled in a lot higher circles than Daisy aspired to. He didn't frequent the all-male sanctuary of the back room at Cut 'N' Chat like some of the drivers and team members did. His haircuts probably cost what Daisy made in a day. He was rich and powerful, a dozen or so years older than Sheila and he could trace his family history back to the Mayflower or close, anyway. *A younger version of August Carlyle.* The comparison sent a shiver down her spine.

"Gil's a nice guy," Mellie said decisively. "I approve of him."

"Coming from you, that's a great recommendation." Daisy didn't know a lot about what had happened in Mellie's life before she came to Mooresville, but she had her suspicions it hadn't been an easy one. Her friend didn't trust people easily. Gil Sizemore certainly didn't seem like the type to appeal to the down-to-earth, hardworking Sheila but there was no accounting for the laws of attraction, and if Mellie approved of him, Daisy would stop worrying about Sheila's taste in men.

"Hey, look at the TV," Sheila said, as much to change the subject as to call their attention to the NASCAR history unfolding on the giant screen above the fireplace. "There's Bart and his brother, Will, back when they were both driving in the Camping World Truck Series. Get a look at those haircuts. I swear Will's sporting a mullet!"

"No way." Mellie giggled, swiveling her head toward the TV. "Millionaire playboys? Is that what the headline under the picture says? Is that true?"

"It's true or used to be, anyway. Their father was enormously rich but he embezzled a lot a money from his stockholders a couple of years ago and the family lost just about everything, including Bart and Will's car sponsorships. It was a really big deal. Especially when their dad up and disappeared like he did. Took the police, gosh, over a year to track him down," Daisy informed the other two women.

"Who's that man with them?" Mellie asked. She wasn't paying attention to Lily smearing PB&J all over her fingers, or that her own fork was poised halfway to her mouth with a cherry tomato from the pasta salad speared on the end.

Daisy glanced up at the screen, narrowing her eyes a little to bring the grainy newspaper photo being displayed over the narrative into better focus. "That's him, their dad, Hilton Branch. He's in prison now and probably will be for the rest of his life." The image faded into a more recent picture of Bart and Will trading high-fives after they finished 1-2 at Pocono back in June.

"Hilton Branch?"

"You look like you've seen a ghost," Sheila said to Mellie as she reached over the table to wipe Lily's sticky fingers with a handful of paper napkins she'd brought from the kitchen.

Sheila was exaggerating about Mellie looking as if she'd seen a ghost, but her young friend was definitely upset about something. Was it the fact that Bart's father was a convicted felon? It would certainly be a shock for Daisy if she found that out about a guy she was interested in. "I'm sorry I just blurted it out that way, Mellie, about Bart's dad being in prison, I mean."

"Don't apologize, Daisy." Mellie's voice sounded strained. "Bart and I are just acquaintances from the diner. Why would he tell me any of this kind of embarrassing family stuff?" Mellie stabbed another tomato from her plate. Her hands were trembling. "Let's talk about something else, okay?"

Sheila and Daisy exchanged a puzzled look. Sheila lifted her shoulders in a shrug and did as Mellie asked. "With what's leftover here you'll have plenty to eat for the next few days. We'll take turns popping out to look in on you two over the weekend."

"You don't have to do that," Daisy protested, waving her hand palm out, like a traffic cop. "I'll be fine here with Quinn…and Brianna," she added hastily. Goodness, why had she phrased it that way, putting Quinn ahead of her daughter?

Sheila gave her a considering look. "Oh, I assumed Quinn would be going to Atlanta for the race. He's probably got sponsor obligations. Atlanta's a big market for sports drinks."

"I…we…he hasn't said anything about leaving." Daisy knew her face was turning red. It hadn't occurred to her that Quinn was neglecting his business by staying out here for so long. It seemed he was always on the computer, or talking on his cell phone during the day. She had just assumed he could conduct all his business that way. How silly and naive of her. "But even if he does go to Atlanta, Brianna and I will be just fine on our own. We've got everything we need and y'all are just a phone call away."

"I want to go home," Lily complained.

Mellie glanced at the cheap watch on her wrist. "Oh, dear, it is almost two. I can't believe we've been here so long. You must be worn-out."

Daisy laughed, reluctant to see her friends go. "I'm fine. I had a quick nap before you got here. You learn to take them when you can get them when there's a baby in the house."

"Don't I know it," Mellie said. Her friend seemed to have regained her good humor. Daisy put the talk about the Branch scandal out of her mind and began piling up dirty dishes for Sheila to take into the kitchen.

She held Lily on her lap and listened to the three-year-old's nonstop prattle, thinking that someday Brianna would be this bright and chatty and that it would probably happen much sooner than she planned. Brianna woke up fussing just as Sheila and Mellie came back into the living room.

"She's hungry," Lily announced, wiggling off Daisy's lap to run to Mellie. "Daisy says next time we come I can hold her."

Brianna's cries grew louder.

"Stay sitting," Sheila ordered. "I'll have a bottle ready in a jiffy." She disappeared back into the kitchen.

"She's impatient when it's time to eat," Daisy said, smiling down at her wide-awake daughter. "Every three hours like clockwork. I wish I could stretch it out to four but she just won't hear of it."

"Maybe just a tiny bit of rice cereal mixed with her formula on the tip of a spoon," Mellie suggested, lifting Brianna out of the carrier, giving her a hug and a kiss on top of her head before handing her to Daisy. "I know a lot of doctors don't believe in solid foods this early but it worked wonders for Lily. She was such a fussy baby."

"Maybe I will try it," Daisy said. She'd call her mother after her friends left and get her recommendation, after all Lelah Brookshire had raised four children of her own and had watched over Daisy's niece and nephew, her divorced oldest brother's children, since they were babies, too.

"Babies are tougher than you think. If she doesn't like it she'll let you know soon enough," Mellie said with a laugh. "C'mon, Lily, time to get you home and ready to go to Louise's." Lily's babysitter, a wonderful woman who just happened to be the wife of the cook at Maudie's, had also agreed to watch over Brianna when Daisy went back to work at Cut 'N' Chat.

"Here we go," Sheila said, returning with the bottle. She handed it to Daisy and moments later Brianna's cries were replaced with loud sucking noises.

"That's better." Lily took her hands away from her ears. Everyone laughed.

"Let's go," Mellie said, swinging Lily into her arms. Daisy remained seated. She would love to walk her friends to the car but she still didn't trust her footing in the rutted driveway and overgrown yard.

"Call us if there's anything at all you need—or want," Sheila said in her usual forceful, I-won't-take-no-for-an-answer tone. "Anything at all."

"I will," Daisy promised, secretly pleased that she had friends who cared so much about her. "But, really, I'll be fine."

She would be, too, except she would miss Quinn a whole lot more than she was comfortable admitting.

CHAPTER EIGHT

"I THINK WE SHOULD LOOK into franchising your friend Sheila's meat loaf," Quinn said, leaning back in his chair as he surveyed his empty plate. "We could all become very, very rich making people all over the country deliriously happy at mealtime."

Daisy laughed. "You're already rich," she said teasingly, before she could stop herself.

"Only on paper," Quinn replied.

Daisy felt her cheeks turn hot and it wasn't because she had her hands in soapy dishwater. "I'm sorry, that was rude. Please forgive me." She had spoken to him as if they were old friends who knew everything about each other and could poke fun at each other, instead of near strangers who had been thrown together by circumstance and necessity.

"It's okay, Daisy. I do have a lot of material assets but I'm not in the same league as my stepfather."

"And my criteria for considering someone filthy rich are extremely low," she quipped, trying to make light of her gaffe. "Right now I'd call three months rent in the bank and a paid-for car being on Easy Street. Still, your financial situation is none of my business. It was a little joke…a very little joke."

"I can take a joke," he said, setting his plate and silverware on the drain board. "You don't have to hang your head for bringing up the fact I have money."

"Okay, I forgive myself." She attempted a smile but she

thought it might have come off a little ragged around the edges. Now everything felt awkward again because she still felt guilty about keeping him chained to the cabin when he had more important things to do than fetch and carry for her and her daughter.

She turned back to washing Brianna's bottles with fierce concentration. She had allowed herself to be lulled into a false feeling of intimacy, of sharing, almost of family, these past days of near total isolation with Quinn. Sheila must have passed the word to her friends and the Tuesday Tarts because their vigilance had dwindled off into phone calls and text messages instead of daily visits.

It had been just the two of them and the baby for the past three days.

Quinn had declared he was taking the Labor Day weekend off to do just that—labor—at the farm. He had spent all of Friday and Saturday working to bring the junglelike yard under control. He'd rented a big, heavy-duty riding mower and scrounged around in the barn until he came up with rakes and hoes and a wheelbarrow that was in surprisingly good shape once the tire was pumped up. He'd trimmed and pruned and rooted out dead wood until he had a big pile of brush. After Brianna had fallen asleep in her lacy bassinette Daisy came outside on the porch to sit and watch the flames.

Quinn had joined her after fetching a beer from the kitchen, rocking in the chair beside hers as the embers glowed with shades of orange and red and overhead stars blinked into life. It was quiet in the clearing where they sat, but far away, out on the lake, the sound of fishing boats starting their engines to head back into shore for the night came very faintly to their ears. It had been like a little slice of heaven for Daisy, those quiet hours; the kind of life she had privately envisioned for herself when she was with Brendan, although she had always known that a simple cabin in the woods was not his style.

If only she had met someone like Quinn first. She had been foolish to fall in love with Brendan. He was charming and outgoing, but she had learned to her sorrow there was little depth of character and maturity in the man behind the smiling facade. She would never give her heart that easily again. Daisy sighed and ran the bottle under a stream of hot water to rinse it before setting it upside down in the rack.

"Now what's wrong?" Quinn asked, leaning one hip against the counter, folding his arms across his chest while he studied her profile. She would never in a million years admit to her thoughts because she didn't want to hurt his feelings by speaking ill of his dead stepbrother, or admit that she also felt a sense of relief that she wouldn't have to share her daughter with a man she couldn't respect, and no longer loved.

"I wish you'd gone to Atlanta," she said, bringing up another point that had been bothering her. "Brianna and I would have been fine here alone."

"Is that why you've been so touchy the last day or two? Because I decided to let my partner wine and dine the Atlanta employees at the race track instead of going myself?"

"That's your job," she said. "You told me he was the brains and you were the marketing. The people you'd be entertaining are your regional sales force, right? You should be there."

"Look, that's true, but Zach's not some kind of pencil-necked geek who never leaves the lab. He's been running the family business since he got out of college. He can handle schmoozing with the salesmen as well as I can. Besides, he's a huge NASCAR fan so it's not exactly hardship duty for him."

"Still—"

"How about ice cream?" he asked abruptly, routing the

conversation in a new direction. He grabbed the dish towel from her hand and spun her around, slowly, so she didn't stumble on her still weak ankle and untied the old-fashioned cotton apron she'd found in a kitchen drawer. It was the first time he'd touched her, actually laid hands on her, since he'd carried her into the cabin ten days ago. She shivered a little when she felt his grip on her waist. His hands were as warm and strong as she remembered and just as arousing.

Now where had that extraordinary thought come from? Arousing? She wasn't beginning to think of Quinn that way, in a sexual, man-woman way, was she? She couldn't. She wouldn't.

He tapped the tip of her nose with his finger. "Hey, are you okay? You went a little blank on me there for a moment."

"What? No. I'm fine, just a little dizzy. I'm sorry, what did you say?" she stuttered, shocked to her core to realize that, yes, she was beginning to think of him as more than just a friend, a benefactor. She was beginning to think of him as a man, and a sexy desirable one at that.

"Ice cream. I asked you if you'd like to go for ice cream."

"Ice cream sounds good." It took a lot of willpower to get the words to come out just right but she managed.

"Soft serve in a waffle cone, or maybe a milkshake?" He grinned like a little boy. "Nope, I want a hot fudge sundae. I haven't had one of those in years."

"I love hot fudge sundaes, but we just finished supper."

His grin turned crafty. "It's dessert. If we hurry we can get down to Bubba's Bait & Ice Cream Shop and back before the race starts."

Daisy laughed, her heartbeat settling back into something resembling a normal rhythm. "You're kidding. It's not Bubba's Bait Shop & Ice Cream Parlor for real?"

"Wanna' bet?" Quinn asked, raising one dark eyebrow as if daring her to question his honesty.

"Really?"

"I swear." He held up one hand. "Get Brianna into her carrier and I'll show you."

"Okay," Daisy said, trying her best not to let him see how breathless she'd suddenly become just because he'd smiled at her. He didn't smile often but every time he did it set her heart to hammering in her chest or took her breath away, or sometimes both. "But I'm buying," she said firmly.

"Deal," he replied. "Let's get going. The race starts in less than an hour." He didn't argue and she found it no longer surprised her that he wasn't intimidated by a woman taking the initiative now and then. The day Brianna was born and the days that followed he had been so forceful, so intimidating she had assumed, wrongly, it seemed, that despite his assertions to the contrary, August Carlyle must have been a bigger influence on him growing up than he would admit.

She was very glad she had been wrong about that.

"I'll be ready in a jiff," she said. The Labor Day race was under the lights. If Eli Ward, Quinn's driver, finished in the top ten he would most likely move up enough in the points standings to make the Chase. Her favorite driver was Rafael O'Bryan, who was already locked into one of the top twelve spots for the final run to the championship, but today she was going to root for the No. 502 car with all her heart.

CHAPTER NINE

QUINN AWOKE FROM A LIGHT doze. Was it the far-off rumble of thunder across the lake that had roused him? He looked around the darkened living room. Rain pattered on the roof and tapped against the windows as lightning flickered above the trees. He remembered nights like this when he had lived here with his grandparents. He had always enjoyed the sound of rain on the roof, but that wasn't what had wakened him.

He stretched, running his hands through his hair and listened to the silence. There it was again, the rustling of sound and the faint mewling cry of a newborn.

Brianna was awake.

He glanced over at the couch where Daisy was curled up under one of his grandmother's crocheted afghans sound asleep. He checked the luminous dial of his watch to find it was a few minutes shy of three o'clock. The race had ended just before midnight due to a lengthy red flag delay for a single-car crash that had taken out four other cars as collateral damage. Thankfully none of them had been the Rev Energy Drinks car. In fact Eli had taken the lead soon after the restart and cruised to an easy win. His first in a NASCAR Sprint Cup car. Quinn caught himself grinning again as he remembered the jolt of pride seeing the Rev car in Victory Lane had produced deep in his gut.

He just wished Daisy had been awake to share it with.

She had fallen asleep during the delay and he hadn't had the heart to wake her. It wasn't often that Brianna slept more than three hours at a time, but she had tonight. Maybe it was the cereal Daisy had started feeding her after a lengthy phone conversation with her mother in Florida?

He hadn't realized that changing a newborn's diet was the equivalent to a major corporate marketing decision but he wouldn't make that mistake again. There had been calls to Daisy's mother in Florida, to friends and customers at the salon soliciting advice, a consultation with a nurse manning the New Mother hotline at the hospital, a conference call with Juliana and Patsy Grosso and Patsy's daughter, celebrity chef Grace Winters who had three children of her own, and he had no idea how many others that took place when he wasn't within earshot. The consensus had been to give the feedings a try and so yesterday they had made the trip to Mooresville to the grocery to buy a single box of rice cereal.

It had been quite a production what with diaper bags and an insulated carrier for bottles of formula, and a tote with changes of clothes for both Daisy and her daughter. She'd laughed, shaking her head. "I know, I know it looks as if we're preparing to go around the world and not just to the grocery." Daisy giggled. "But I honestly don't know what I will and won't need yet. Bear with me. By next month I will have the hang of this motherhood thing."

She would, too, Quinn thought indulgently, levering himself up from the chair. He had underestimated Daisy those first couple of days. He had thought she was weak and easily managed, but he had been wrong. She had agreed to his high-handed ordering of her life, was still agreeing to his insistence that she stay at the cabin instead of attempting to return to her third-floor walk-up for Brianna's sake if not her own, but it wasn't because she was weak or malleable.

It was because she was using her head and her common sense to make decisions concerning her baby's welfare and her own. When she was strong enough her innate self-confidence would reassert itself; she would veto any further arguments he might put forward to keep her and Brianna here with him and return to her life and her job and her friends.

And he would be alone again, solitary, as he had always been and, if he was completely honest with himself, even lonelier than he'd been before.

He walked to the bassinette and leaned over to see if Brianna was awake or merely fussing in her sleep. Bright, dark eyes stared back at him from the shadowy interior. She was very definitely wide-awake. So much for hoping he could give her a few pats on the back and she would drop off again.

"Hello, little one," he said very softly. "Are you hungry?" Her hands waved in the air in reply. After a couple of false starts she found her mouth and started sucking her thumb. She was getting good at that. Daisy was already taking suggestions on how to break her of the habit.

"Okay, I'll have to wake your mom, though." He hadn't yet attempted to feed her. He glanced over at Daisy still sound asleep, her hand under her cheek. She looked comfortable and relaxed curled up in the corner of the couch and he hated to wake her. She still had faint shadows beneath her eyes and she needed a long stretch of unbroken rest. Maybe it was time for him to take another step as a surrogate father and feed Brianna himself.

He straightened up and prepared to head for the kitchen. Brianna was having none of that. Her thumb popped out of her mouth and she began to sniffle. He saw her take a big breath and knew she was getting ready to let loose with a real howl. Automatically he bent forward again and picked her up. She squirmed a little against his shoulder, rooting around until she was comfortable, then settled with her tiny face tucked against his neck, her fingers curled around the collar of his shirt.

Quinn stood quietly savoring the moment, dumbstruck by the depth of emotion the tiny, helpless infant stirred to life inside him. He wanted to protect her, to make everything perfect for her for the rest of her life, and not just because she was Brendan's daughter, but because he was falling in love with her himself.

And if he was falling in love with Brianna, what were his feelings for her mother? Was he falling in love with Daisy, too?

He had no idea. In all his thirty-three years he had never been in love, never felt so deeply for any of the women he'd been involved with that he couldn't imagine his life without them. It wasn't that way with Daisy. He had no problem at all imagining how bleak a future without her in it would be. No problem at all.

"OH DEAR, WHAT TIME IS IT?" Daisy sat up, disoriented to find herself still on the couch in the living room. She must have fallen asleep as the delay after the multicar pileup postponed the end of the race past midnight. One moment she had been listening to an on-track announcer interviewing Bart Branch as he sat in his car on the track and the next she had been dreaming of eating ice cream on a rickety dock by the lake, laughing at something funny Quinn had said while Brianna, all grown up, sat beside him eating an ice-cream cone of her own. The warm, fuzzy residue of that idyllic dream faded as time and place returned abruptly. "Brianna?" Her eyes flew to the bassinette. It was empty.

She swung her feet to the floor, wincing as her still-tender ankle bumped against the leg of the low pine table where she and Sheila and Mellie and Lily had held their impromptu inside picnic just a couple of days earlier. "Quinn?" She rose, still a little stiff, and threw the afghan Quinn must have covered her with over the back of the couch.

"Right here," he spoke quietly from across the room.

Brianna was tucked against his shoulder, supported there by one big hand across her back. One of her bottles was stuck in his pants pocket drawing his jeans tight across his narrow hips. Her eyes lingered there for a moment longer than was necessary and she was glad it was dark enough in the big room, lit only by the embers of the small fire Quinn had kindled earlier to help take the dampness from the night air, so that he couldn't see her blush.

She had been noticing more and more of those sorts of sensual details as the days passed and she watched him work out of doors and around the house. He didn't do manual labor for a living but he wasn't a soft man, not by any means. His muscles were well defined. He had broad shoulders and a strong back and although his touch was gentle his hands were as hard and strong as the rest of him.

"I didn't hear her wake up," she said, feeling alarmed she'd slept so deeply. A little arrow of uneasiness streaked through her heart. What if this happened when they were alone together, just the two of them? And what might happen when Brianna was older as she had been in her dream? What if she wandered out of the apartment and out in to traffic?

"You didn't hear her because she didn't make any noise," Quinn assured her and she knew, he had read her thoughts as he seemed to be able to do now and then. "She was awake so I took her with me to warm her bottle. She was bored lying in the bassinette. She wanted to know how the race ended." He settled into the chair at a right angle to where she sat on the couch and began feeding her daughter. It was the first time he'd attempted the task, but he looked as if he'd been doing it all his life.

"I've been taking notes," he said with that devastatingly sexy smile he used so rarely. "I figured it was time I gave it a try."

Daisy found the sight of Brianna in his arms every bit as appealing in real life as it had been in her dreams. Quinn

Parrish would make a wonderful father, a better father than his stepbrother would have been. She didn't berate herself for the thought. It was the truth and she would be less than honest if she pretended otherwise.

"You're doing great." She curled her legs under her and wrapped her arms around a throw pillow, allowing the fantasy of the three of them as a family to play out a little longer.

"She's hungry," he said, looking down at the baby, "but not starving like she always seemed to be before."

Daisy glanced at the clock. "Is it really after three? I fed her at eleven. That's over four hours. Starting her on cereal was the right thing to do, I guess."

"Yeah, it seems that way." He grinned down at Brianna, who was wide-awake and listening to every word, it seemed. "Your momma's a smart lady, isn't she?"

Daisy's throat tightened with emotion. They looked so right together, the two of them. She stiffened, searching for a way to divert her thoughts from going further down a forbidden path. She owed Quinn so much she could never repay. She didn't dare start letting herself think that there could be more to their relationship than gratitude and friendship. That way promised nothing but heartbreak.

"Who won the race?" she asked. The race was a much safer topic of conversation.

"I recorded the finish." Quinn nodded toward the remote as Brianna sucked hungrily on her bottle and grinned. "I think you'll like the way it turned out."

Daisy wondered if she should remind him to burp Brianna now that her formula was half gone, but he glanced at the bottle as he spoke and gently tugged it out of her mouth, lifting her back to his shoulder. The baby squirmed a little, not wanting to stop eating, but after a dozen gentle pats she relaxed and turned her head to nuzzle his neck.

Daisy's heart turned over in her chest and tears stung her

eyes. She fumbled for the remote and switched on the TV to keep from staring at the two of them. She found the right button and began to fast forward through the race delay. The sound was muted. She continued to watch the screen as she talked so he wouldn't see how close she was to losing control of her emotions. "Have you always been a NASCAR fan?" she asked.

"Not when I was a kid," he admitted. "Grandma and Granddad weren't all that much into racing, probably because of my dad's accident, but once my mom married Carlyle and I got old enough to be interested in cars I got hooked. What about you?"

"My dad and my uncle loved dirt track racing. When I was a kid my uncle crewed on a couple of teams but my dad worked two jobs to keep all of us in sneakers and jeans so he didn't have a lot of time or money left over for going to races."

"Did he teach you to drive? You handled your car like a pro that first day I met you."

"Until I pulled out in front of a truck, you mean?" she asked, giving him a quick, rueful glance before turning back to the screen.

"It was an accident, not bad driving."

"The outcome was the same." She shrugged not wanting to think about the accident and how much more serious it could have been for both her and her daughter. "My oldest brother taught me to drive. He always wanted to be a NASCAR driver. He had to settle for driving a big rig."

"He lives near your parents in Florida?"

They had spoken briefly of her family now and then but very little of his. "Mom and Dad moved to Sarasota when Dad's plant closed. They're close by each other. Mom helps out with his kids. My other brother and my sister are in Georgia and Texas. We're scattered all over the place these days." Tears pricked behind her eyelids again. She was still way too emotional. "You're lucky to be near your mother," she said before she could censor her tongue.

"Distance isn't always measured in miles." Brianna emitted a loud unladylike burp and he gave a short bark of laughter. "Way to go, Bri, honey. That was a good one." He settled her back into his arms and began feeding her again. Obviously there wasn't going to be any more discussion about his family.

Daisy pretended to watch the race as the cars fired their engines and took up position for the double-file restart. She hated to see people estranged from their loved ones. There were so many separations, like Brendan's death, that could never be altered or made right. To her way of thinking it was almost a sin to create them among the living. The estrangement between Quinn and his mother was none of her business even though she wished there was something she could do or say to help mend the relationship.

She turned her face away from the screen and looked at Quinn, at the hard, unyielding line of his jaw and knew she couldn't say what was in her heart. Not now, perhaps not ever. He glanced up and caught her watching him. "Don't worry about me, Daisy," he said quietly, leaning forward to touch her cheek with the tips of his fingers. His touch was light and fleeting but its effect on Daisy's nerve endings was anything but. She held herself very still to keep from giving into the temptation to lean into his hand, snuggling against his palm just as Brianna was nestled against his shoulder. The caress seemed to take Quinn by surprise as much as it had her. He dropped his hand and sat back abruptly. Brianna squirmed against his shoulder disturbed by his sudden movement. Automatically he began to pat her back. "It's been this way between the two of us for a long time," he said gruffly. "I'm used to it."

"I'm sorry to hear that." She couldn't hold his gaze. There was darkness in his eyes and sorrow that she knew instinctively he didn't want her to see. The subject of his relationship with his mother was one he didn't intend to pursue. She would respect his wishes even though her heart was heavy with sorrow. She took a quick, steadying breath, forcing her mind away from the shattering impact of his touch. She raised the volume on the TV slightly so that they wouldn't have to sit in silence, but not loud enough that the sound of the big engines roaring to life would startle Brianna who had settled once more. "So," she said with false brightness. "Tell me where Eli finished in case I fall asleep again."

CHAPTER TEN

BY TUESDAY THE RAIN had ended and the heat of early September had returned. Quinn was getting ready to go into Charlotte to take care of a number of things at the office that had been waiting his attention through the long holiday weekend. She and Brianna were going with him as far as Mooresville where they would spend the afternoon holding court at Cut 'N' Chat and then, if Brianna wasn't too fussy, they would join the Tarts for their regular evening at Maudie's Down Home Diner.

Daisy was relieved to be spending the day on her own. She couldn't seem to get the memory of Quinn's fleeting caress out of her thoughts or her dreams. It was the starting point for a whole series of intimate, sensual imaginings that told her she was much closer to falling in love with him than she had ever thought she would be.

She had no idea how he felt about her.

She knew she was going to have to leave this secluded cabin soon. The realization saddened her more than she wanted to admit. It was definitely time to go, to get her life back under her own control. Today she would make plans with Rue and Sheila to return to her apartment. Her ankle was still not as strong as she would like it to be but she couldn't stay here, alone, with Quinn any longer. Not if she didn't want to fall completely and helplessly in love with him and end up with a broken heart.

"Ready to go?" he asked coming out of the kitchen with the small insulated cooler she used for Brianna's bottles.

"Ready." She gave him a blinding smile that probably looked as manufactured as it felt and held up her tote. "Everything we need for a girls' day out on the town." It had taken her almost half an hour to pack everything she thought was essential to her daughter's comfort. Soon she wouldn't have the luxury of spending ten minutes picking out just the right outfit, deciding on which receiving blanket was the best match for the little pink jumper with the tiny bunnies embroidered on the front, whether to dress her daughter in the crocheted booties or the tiny white shoes and lacy anklets. She wanted to savor every moment.

"I brought the car around while you were getting Brianna ready." He reached for Brianna's carrier.

Daisy shook her head. "I'll do it," she said. "My ankle's almost healed. It's time I got used to carrying her."

Quinn frowned. "Are you sure? The yard's still pretty rough."

"I'm sure," Daisy said firmly. She had made her decision in the sleepless hours before dawn. She was going home, soon. She had no other choice.

His eyebrows drew together as his frown deepened. Was he reading her thoughts again? It didn't matter. He would know soon enough that she was leaving for good.

"Daisy—"

"We'd better get started. You've got plenty of work to catch up on before the weekend." Quinn was going to Richmond for the last race before the Chase for the NASCAR Sprint Cup began. Eli Ward was on the bubble, thirteenth in points. A good finish Sunday would move him up in the standings and qualify him for the ten-race Chase. He would leave for Virginia on Friday morning.

She would leave on Thursday. It would be better that way.

"We need to talk," he said, retaining his grip on Brianna's carrier. "We need to talk about—"

"This evening," she said, hurriedly. She wanted to have all her options laid out, all her arguments ready or she was afraid she would weaken and give in to the growing desire, the growing need inside her, to stay, here, with Quinn.

"Not this evening," he said forcefully. "Now—" A knock on the door stopped him in mid-sentence. "Are you expecting anyone this morning?"

Daisy shook her head, suddenly apprehensive. It had been so peaceful and she felt so secure in Quinn's company she had almost forgotten the danger August Carlyle's threats posed to her and her child. She looked past Quinn's shoulder, alarmed to see a sleek, black sports car parked behind Quinn's SUV. "Don't open the door," she said, giving voice to her fears.

It was too late. Quinn had already set Brianna's carrier down on the couch and opened the door. His broad shoulders blocked Daisy's view. Acting on instinct she reached down and picked up the sleeping baby, holding her tight against her heart. "Who is it, Quinn?" she asked.

He didn't answer her but spoke directly to the person on the other side of the screen. "Mom, what are you doing here?"

His mother? Daisy relaxed a tiny fraction, not really certain why, only that her greatest fear, that it was August Carlyle himself standing on the porch, had not come true. She reached out and touched Quinn's arm. He moved out of the doorway but didn't invite his mother inside.

Fiona Carlyle's gaze was locked on Brianna's face as she slept against Daisy's shoulder. The cool, composed expression she usually wore dissolved into softness. "She looks so much like the pictures I've seen of Brendan at that age," she whispered and Daisy saw the shimmer of tears in the older woman's eyes.

Eyes almost exactly the same incredible blue of Quinn's.

Daisy was a mother now and she sensed the older woman's emotional response to Brianna was real. Fiona Carlyle was a mother grieving for a lost child, not her flesh and blood, it was true, but a child of her heart. This woman had lost part of herself when Brendan died, and she had nothing left of him but memories. And adding to that burden of grief was her estrangement from her own son. Sadness and pity welled up inside Daisy. She made a decision she hoped she would not regret and reached past Quinn to open the screen door. "Come in, Mrs. Carlyle," she said, taking a step back.

"Thank you." Fiona Carlyle was dressed as expensively and impeccably as she had been the day she and her husband came to the hospital, but beneath the flawless makeup Daisy saw strain and the dark shadows of sleepless nights.

"What do you want, Mom?" Quinn asked. Daisy was standing close enough to feel the waves of tension radiating from him although his voice betrayed no emotion beyond politeness.

Fiona made an effort to tear her eyes away from Brianna. She clasped her hands around her designer shoulder bag— one that Daisy knew for a fact would cost her more than a week's salary and tips—and faced her son. Her expression didn't change when she encountered his cool indifference but she stuttered slightly, betraying her inner turmoil. "I...I came to see the baby. To see Brendan's little girl."

"Does August know you're here?"

Fiona lifted her chin, as though she had had enough of his cross-examination, and Daisy recognized a feminine version of Quinn's stubbornness in the gesture. "No, I came on my own."

"I'm surprised you stepped that far out of line," Quinn said darkly.

"I don't always tell your stepfather everything I do," she

returned, but Daisy could see the words had hit a vulner-able spot.

"Quinn, let your mother say what she came to say," Daisy interrupted.

"Thank you. I don't wish you any harm, Daisy. I just wanted to ask you to meet with my husband and try to work something out between you."

Daisy shook her head. "I don't think that's possible. I'm sorry but I don't trust your husband at all."

"He's not a bad man, just one that is used to getting his own way. Losing Brendan was a terrible blow to my husband. Brianna is all that he has left of his son." Fiona looked to Quinn as if hoping against hope that he might agree with her. He remained silent and Fiona seemed to wilt a little under his impassive stare. "This wasn't a good idea, me coming out here, was it?" she said finally.

Daisy didn't want to feel sorry for Quinn's mother. It was so much easier to stay strong when her heart was filled with anger and righteous indignation toward both the Car-lyles. She didn't want to start thinking about Fiona's loss, her heartache, all that she would miss out on in her grandchild's life, but she couldn't retreat. Fiona might not be as much of a danger as she had thought before but she was convinced August still was. "I won't change my mind," she said as much to herself as to Fiona. "Never."

Brianna started to fuss, sensing Daisy's distress. Fiona broke eye contact with Daisy and returned her stricken gaze to the baby. "Please," she said, "may I hold her, just for a moment?"

Daisy wanted to say no. Her own mother hadn't held Brianna yet, so why should she let this woman? *Because Fiona had loved Brianna's father and lost him and grieved for him,* her inner voice prompted. Daisy was a mother now; she understood these things. Fiona deserved the comfort of holding Brendan's child. "Yes," Daisy said. "You may hold her."

Fiona smiled and held out her arms, but before Daisy could hand her the baby, a second car, almost as expensive as the one Fiona drove, pulled into the yard and a short, compact man in a dark suit exited the driver's side. He was carrying a briefcase. Even though Daisy had never seen him before she knew instinctively he was a lawyer, and his being here could mean nothing but trouble.

"What do you want?" she asked, stepping up to the screen but not opening it. The lawyer stood on the other side, aloof and detached although she noticed that laugh lines fanned out from the corners of his eyes and mouth, or perhaps they weren't laugh lines, but only the result of hours spent playing golf in the hot Carolina sun.

"I'm here to see Deidre Brookshire. May I come in?"

"No," Quinn said sharply, moving to stand close behind Daisy. "What do you want?"

"I have a communication from my client, August Carlyle." The stranger's gaze flickered to Fiona for a moment then confronted Daisy again.

"What does he want?" Daisy asked, proud that her voice came out strong and steady despite the way her knees were shaking. She could feel Quinn's warmth and rock solidness behind her and it helped steady her to have him so close, even though two weeks earlier he had been as much a stranger as the man on the other side of the screen.

"Mr. Carlyle is giving you one more opportunity to meet with him and his representatives to make arrangements for the future well-being of his grandchild. If you do not agree to such a meeting he intends to go to Child Protective Services and file a complaint. It is my client's sincere belief that you, an unmarried, single woman of modest means and education cannot properly care for his granddaughter."

"That's not true," Daisy said, tightening her grip on

Brianna so that the baby woke, startled and began to cry. "That's not true at all. I have a good job. I can take good care of my baby."

"That remains to be seen," the lawyer said in a voice whose very blandness made it even more of a threat than if he had shouted at the top of his lungs. "I take it you're rejecting my client's offer of a meeting without even giving him the courtesy of hearing what he is prepared to offer you and your daughter?"

"I am."

"Leave the paperwork," Quinn said. "Ms. Brookshire will look it over. If she changes her mind we'll be in touch."

The lawyer switched his gaze to Quinn, hesitated a moment as if hoping he might intimidate the younger man, then nodded. "Very well." He took a legal-size envelope out of the briefcase and laid it on the seat of the rocking chair nearest the door. "Ms. Brookshire, may I give you a piece of advice?"

Daisy wanted nothing more than to slam the door in the man's face but that childish gesture, no matter how satisfying, wouldn't solve anything. "I don't suppose I can stop you," she said, proud that her voice didn't waver.

"It would be in your daughter's best interest, indeed in your own best interests, to meet with August Carlyle. You are a young woman alone in the world. You don't have the means to fight a man with my client's resources and standing in the community. You are in very real danger of eventually losing custody of your daughter. Think about it."

"I think about it all the time," Daisy said, holding on to her courage as tightly as she held her baby. "But it won't change my mind. Please, leave us alone." This time she did shut the door in the man's face.

She turned blindly. Her knees were shaking so hard she was afraid they would fold under her and topple them both to the floor. Quinn was watching her from narrowed eyes, his hands balled into fists at his side, but it was Fiona Carlyle's white, strained gaze that locked with hers. Daisy took a half-step backward. The last few minutes had been so emotionally charged, her attention focused so completely on the confrontation with August Carlyle's lawyer that she had momentarily forgotten his wife had been witness to it.

"I…I think you should go, too," she said. Her head was pounding, her pulse racing with a surge of adrenaline. Fight or flight, didn't they call it? The lawyer was right. She couldn't fight August Carlyle and come out ahead so she would have to go. Leave Mooresville and Cut 'N' Chat and her friends.

Leave Quinn.

"Daisy, please, I knew nothing about this, you have to believe me." Fiona took a step forward, her hand outstretched. Daisy kept her teeth clamped shut. Did she believe Fiona? Could her husband have been planning something so monstrous as trying to have her declared an unfit mother without his wife knowing about it? "Quinn?" Fiona turned beseeching eyes on her son.

Quinn returned her look with one as hard as stone. "Daisy's right. I think you'd better go, Mom," he said.

"Quinn, you believe me, don't you?"

"I'd like to, Mom," he said. His expression was still hard but his voice had gentled slightly. "But even if you didn't know he was planning this you wouldn't have tried to stop him. You never have before."

"Quinn—" She covered her mouth with her hand as though to hold back a sob. "I'll make this right," she said, turning to Daisy again. "I swear to you I'll make this right."

Daisy didn't answer. She didn't dare. "Please, just go," she said wearily. She stepped away from the door. "Now."

Fiona lifted her hand in a gesture of defeat. She no longer looked cool and detached. She looked as if she'd aged ten years. "Of course, I'll go. But I will make this right," she said. "For Brendan's sake and for my own."

Fiona walked outside, her back straight and proud, and shut the door quietly behind her. A moment later Daisy heard her car drive away. The sound of the engine receding in the distance broke the paralysis that had held her still. She looked down at Brianna nestled in the crook of her elbow, her dark eyes wide-open, her tiny face scrunched into a frown that matched the one on Daisy's face.

She touched her finger to Brianna's cheek, let the baby wrap her tiny fingers around her fingertip in a surprisingly strong grip. She took strength from that contact and lifted her face to Quinn's. "I'm going, too," she said. "Now, and for good."

CHAPTER ELEVEN

DAISY LOOKED AS IF SHE WOULD turn on him next if he made even the slightest move toward her. Quinn wanted nothing more than to take her in his arms and hold her close but he stayed where he was, standing with one shoulder propped against the mantelpiece, striving to sound as relaxed as if they were speaking of nothing more important than the chances that the big low pressure system moving up from the south would rain out Saturday night's race.

Daisy continued to eye him as if he might suddenly morph into August Carlyle between one breath and the next. Her elfin features were taut with strain and he could see tremors of nervous reaction coursing through her body. She turned shakily and laid the baby back in her carrier, tucking a blanket snuggly around her. She fastened the safety straps as though she were still making plans for a quick getaway.

"I'll have to ask you to drive me into town," she said. Quinn balled his hands into fists again. This wasn't the moment for him to act on his emotions. She was too close to the ragged edge of panic for him to overload her with declarations…of what? Love? Commitment? He wanted both of those things but he didn't have the words, the right words, not yet, so he stayed put and attempted to be the voice of reason.

"Daisy, slow down. August won't be sending the Child Protective Services people out here in the next fifteen minutes. Sit down before you fall down. You won't do Brianna any good if you pass out on me."

She straightened and gave him a quick, angry glance. "I'm not going to pass out on you."

Good. That was what he wanted, for her fighting spirit to reassert itself. He motioned for her to take a seat beside Brianna's carrier. "Let's talk about this."

"There's nothing to talk about, Quinn." Her tone was argumentative not fearful, another good sign. "I'm leaving here and I'm not coming back. I'll…I'll keep in touch, I promise you." She didn't quite meet his eyes when she spoke and he knew she was lying to him.

Now it was his turn to almost panic. "Daisy, you can't run away," he said, lowering himself into a chair so that he wasn't towering over her. He didn't want her to associate him with his bullying stepfather any more than she already did.

"What else can I do? I can't afford to pay a lawyer to fight for me and I won't take money from you," she said before he could even offer. She picked up one of Brianna's cloth diapers from the pine table and began to fold and refold it over and over again.

"You can't afford to just up and disappear, either. It's exactly what August expects you to do. It's what he wants you to do. You'd be even more vulnerable trying to start over among strangers. You know it and he knows it. We have to take our time, work out a plan, find a lawyer, a good lawyer. They're out there. It's just going to take some time."

"Lawyers are expensive," she repeated stubbornly.

"There are also ones who aren't out to make a billion dollars. Their fees are based on ability to pay, or even pro bono."

"I'm not a charity case, yet. I'll pay what I can." He ran his hand through his hair, torn between exasperation and ex-

hilaration. She was coming around to his way of thinking…
he just had to keep playing it calm and collected.

"I'll make some calls, get you a list of names. You can
take it from there."

"Can you start making calls right away? I don't trust your
stepfather not to go directly to the authorities." She looked
as if she might panic again.

"Daisy, take a deep breath, think this through."

"I don't trust him," she repeated stubbornly.

"Look," he said as if the thought had just occurred to him.
"I know a place you can stay for the next few days where
August won't think of looking for you."

Her chin came up. Her eyes were no longer dulled with
fright. They were clear and bright, the color of melted honey.
He loved her eyes. He was falling in love with everything
about her. "What are you suggesting?"

"You and Brianna are going to Richmond," he said.

"What?"

"You heard me. I have a motor home rented for the week.
It's being set up in one of the VIP areas at the race track
today. I'll make sure it's stocked with food and ready when
you get there."

"I don't have a car. I'm not supposed to drive for at least
another week." She was throwing up obstacles but he knew
she saw the sense in his plan. She had herself under control again. She wasn't going to run, not now, hopefully not
ever.

Quinn let himself relax a little, a fraction of a degree.
"My assistant will drive you. Pack what you need for the trip.
Then we'll go into Mooresville and I'll go on to Charlotte
just like we'd planned. Sheila Trueblood or Rue Larrabee, or
maybe your friend Mellie, can drive you to a rendezvous with
my assistant. You'll be in Richmond before nightfall."

"What about you?" She was leaning forward now, the

diaper still between her hands but she was no longer twisting the cotton rectangle into tortured knots.

"I told you, it will take time to find the right lawyer." That wasn't precisely true. He knew exactly who he was going to ask to take on Daisy's case: an old college friend, who actually did do a lot of pro bono work for single women with child custody problems. He hadn't lied to her, not really; he just hadn't given her all the facts. With Daisy, he'd learned over the past two weeks, you picked your fights.

"I don't know?" She was wavering again, having second thoughts. "Maybe I should just take the bus to Florida. My parents will help me all they can."

"Florida is the first place August will look for you."

"Damn, you're right about that." Quinn remained quiet, letting her work through all the questions and doubts that were circling through her brain. After a few long moments she gave him a sidelong glance and a rueful smile that stampeded his heart rate into overdrive. She looked down at the baby who had fallen asleep sucking her thumb as the tension in the adults abated. When she looked over to him again the smile had disappeared. Her expression was solemn. "I have to handle this myself."

She stood up and Quinn followed suit. She wouldn't be alone much longer if he had any say in the matter, but that was for later. He shoved his hands in his pockets so he didn't reach out and gather her into his arms and undo all the hard work of the last fifteen minutes by overplaying his hand. They hadn't had a date, a first kiss, any sort of romance. He couldn't just come out and tell her he was falling in love with her, but damn it, he was.

"All right, I'll go to Richmond. The last place a snob like August Carlyle would think to look for the runaway mother of his grandchild would be in a motor home at a NASCAR race, right?"

"HEY, SWEETHEART, guess what? It's stopped raining. No really, I'm not kidding." Daisy giggled. Okay. She was talking to a two-week-old infant as if she expected an answer but she was starting to go a little stir-crazy. She picked up her daughter from her nest of blankets on the couch and held her up to the large window in the salon of Quinn's luxurious motor home. "See? The sun's trying to come out. That means there will be a race this evening. Under the lights. They always race under the lights at Richmond."

For the past two days watching raindrops chase each other down the window glass had been the only racing going on at the track. A low pressure system had settled over Virginia, taking its time moving off to sea, but not dampening the spirits of the hardy NASCAR fans.

Not that Daisy had been doing much partying, herself. In fact, the first two days she'd been sequestered in the motor home she'd adapted to Brianna's schedule and slept most of the time. But on Friday morning she was fully rested and happy to find her self-imposed isolation come to an end when Sophia and her mother appeared at her door and insisted Daisy and Brianna join them for brunch, which Milo and Juliana were hosting in their motor home. She didn't even question how the Grosso women had learned of her presence at the track. Rue and Sheila would have informed their sister Tarts of her whereabouts and charged them with looking after her. She just went along with the flow of the day, touched to have such good friends to support her.

After she stuffed herself with homemade cinnamon rolls and fresh fruit Sophia decreed they were going shopping along the line of souvenir haulers, both inside and outside the track. They'd hopped in a gas-powered golf cart and headed out, leaving Brianna with a delighted Juliana, dodging race fans and rain showers. It was the most fun Daisy had had in weeks and she came back with a bib emblazoned with Bart Branch's picture and autograph, and a tiny pair of booties she'd found at one of the Mom and Pop stands in a campground off track, that were crocheted in Rev Energy Drinks' signature colors of green and white and gold.

Quinn had arrived later that afternoon in the middle of a thunderstorm looking sexy and windblown and bearing take-out containers of meat loaf and barbecue from Maudie's in an insulated cooler filled with dry ice. They shared the barbecue and a bottle of good red wine and Daisy felt the tension that had been building inside her the past few days begin to ease away. While they ate and Brianna dozed in her carrier on the couch in the salon, Quinn told her that neither August nor his mother had contacted him since Fiona had left the cabin, but that he had found a lawyer willing to take Daisy's case if it became necessary, and had set up a meeting with her on Monday afternoon after they returned to Mooresville.

But beyond that short time together she had seen him only now and then. He was staying in another motor home in a lot on the other side of the race track with his partner. He kept in touch by cell phone and text message but he had sponsor events planned, commitments to his employees and evenings filled with entertaining dealers and potential new customers.

She told herself she didn't mind the solitude. She felt safe, a modern day princess in a diesel-powered, mobile, enchanted castle, only a little smaller in size than her apartment but light years advanced in style and comfort. Yet, as the weekend wore on she found herself spending more and more time watching and waiting for Quinn to walk in the door and fill their quiet out-of-the-way sanctuary with energy and excitement. The realization of how much she'd come to depend on his companionship and guidance frightened her. It meant she had become far too emotionally involved. She had to put some distance between them soon, or it would be too late. She was already more than half in love with him. It wouldn't take any effort at all to tumble the rest of the way.

By race time Saturday she'd begun talking to herself—or to Brianna, which at this point in her daughter's development amounted to the same thing. "We haven't had a date, he hasn't brought me flowers or candy—or me him, for that matter. We haven't kissed." She shook her head ruefully. "Listen to me telling you all this." She rubbed noses with Brianna who giggled, Daisy was sure of it. "Mommy sounds just like she did in eighth grade when she had a crush on Tyler Whitman and got herself so tied up in knots she couldn't eat or sleep."

Brianna gurgled some more. "No, really, it's true. I was head over heels for him. He was the quarterback on the junior high football team and the cutest guy in my class. Now he weighs two hundred fifty pounds and manages a Piggly Wiggly in Memphis."

Brianna blinked as though attempting to picture her mother's old flame, then began noisily sucking her thumb.

"Of course I'm not having any trouble eating or sleeping," Daisy confessed, gently removing Brianna's thumb from her mouth. She might as well have saved herself the effort because as soon as she let go of her hand back it went. "But Quinn certainly has my insides tied up in knots."

And she had no idea if he felt anything for her at all beyond an obligation to his dead stepbrother's child.

The sudden roar of engines even bigger than those under the hoods of the NASCAR Sprint Cup cars vibrated through the motor home. Brianna kicked her arms and legs and wrinkled her face up to cry. Daisy picked her up, and rocked her in the crook of her arm. "Did those noisy old engines frighten you? It's okay, sweetie. They're just drying the track. It's stopped raining and the race will be starting soon. Quinn will come and get us in a little while and you can go and visit with Nana Grosso." She was going to join Quinn and a dozen or so others in the Rev Energy Drinks suite high above the track to watch the race. Juliana had offered to babysit Brianna and Daisy had said yes.

"It's not like it's a date, or anything," she assured the bright-eyed baby in her arms. "I mean, there will be lots of other people there. I'll just be one of the guests. Just this once," she promised herself, knowing how close to leaving she was. "Just this one evening and then we'll be on our own."

The thought made her want to cry.

A knock on the door sent her heart skating into overdrive. Quinn was early. He wasn't supposed to pick them up for almost half an hour. She hadn't even changed to the slacks and sweater—her regular size, yea!—she'd picked out to wear. She stood up and crossed the salon to the door. Uneasiness replaced the pleasant zing of anticipation she'd been experiencing. It wasn't Quinn's familiar broad-shouldered profile outlined in the frosted glass of the window. There were two people standing there: a woman and a tall, thin man, Fiona and August Carlyle.

They'd found her at last.

CHAPTER TWELVE

"I TOLD YOU I'D BE BACK," Fiona said. She smiled but it wasn't a very good one. Her eyes were filled with trepidation. "I've brought August with me, to explain, to make things right," she added hurriedly as though she expected Daisy to slam the door in their faces. "Please, may we come in?"

Daisy's mind whirled with contradictory thoughts and emotions. She wanted to grab Brianna and run for the other end of the motor home, escape through the back door and find her way to…Quinn. She straightened her shoulders, fighting off the almost overwhelming urge to give in to the impulse. Quinn was at the Double S Racing hauler. He and his partner were meeting with Gil Sizemore to start preliminary negotiations on extending Rev's sponsorship of Eli Ward and the No. 502 car. He wouldn't return for at least half an hour.

She was on her own.

She took a deep breath and stood back from the door. These people were not monsters, she reminded herself. They wouldn't grab Brianna from her arms and flee into the night. She scolded herself for even indulging in such a foolish scenario. She was stronger now, not confined to a hospital bed. She had been on her own since she was eighteen. She could fight for herself and her daughter. She didn't need anyone's help, including Quinn's.

She didn't need his help, but oh, how she wanted it.

"Come in," she said.

Fiona came first, glancing around the salon at the leather furniture and flat screen TV on the wall above the driver's compartment, and then into the kitchen with its marble countertops and gleaming brushed aluminum appliances and the hallway leading to the mirror-walled bedroom. She blinked as if she hadn't quite realized how successful Quinn must be to afford such luxury. Had she really been so out-of-touch with her son the last few years not to know how successful he'd become? How sad. Despite her intention to stay cool and aloof Daisy felt her heart soften toward Quinn's mother.

Fiona was wearing dark slacks and a white silk blouse beneath a black pullover sweater and no jewelry. NASCAR credentials hung from a lanyard around her neck. She wouldn't look out of place in any of the private suites at the race track, if not in the motor home lots and campgrounds surrounding the track. August, on the other hand, looked exactly like who he was: a multimillionaire out of his element. His khaki slacks were creased to a knife point and his blazer was cashmere. He wasn't wearing a tie but the cuff links peeking beneath the sleeves of his jacket were certainly real gold and pawning his watch would keep Brianna in diapers and formula until she was ready to potty-train.

Daisy focused her attention on Brianna's grandfather. "What do you want to say to me, Mr. Carlyle?"

"I came at my wife's insistence to make my peace with you," he said unexpectedly.

Daisy was caught off guard. She had been ready to refer him and his odious list of demands to her lawyer, hand him the woman's card and order him out of the motor home. Now all she could do was stare openmouthed and ask him to repeat himself.

"I came to make peace with you for my wife's sake, and for my granddaughter's sake," he said again.

"I told you I would make him understand," Fiona said, stepping forward to wrap her hands around his right arm.

He lifted his left hand and placed it over hers, looking down at her from his great height. The caress was unstudied and genuinely affectionate.

Daisy recalled what Patsy Grosso, a woman she admired very much, had said about Fiona; that she was a generous person. Patsy liked her. She had raised Quinn to be a strong successful man. She had loved Brendan as though he were her own child. Would she have stayed with a man she didn't love and couldn't trust all these years merely for security? Daisy suddenly didn't think so.

"My wife has brought me to the realization that I have gone about this all the wrong way," August said. His words weren't smooth and polished like the man himself, they were raw with feeling that he seemed to be trying hard to repress. "My methods may have been overreaching but my intentions are good."

Daisy shook her head. She might have been looking at this man through a flawed lens, knowing him only through hearing Brendan's petulant complaints and perhaps, Quinn's equally flawed perspective, but it didn't alter the fact that he had threatened to have Brianna taken away from her. That threat couldn't be ignored; must be dealt with. "You wanted complete control over Brianna's future. You threatened to have her taken away from me."

"That was wrong," Fiona burst out, tears coming to her eyes. "August let his lawyer have too much say in the matter. It won't happen again. Show her, Auggie," she said, abandoning her cultured, composed facade, revealing the raw emotions she'd been keeping inside. "Show her."

August pulled a single sheet of folded paper from the inside pocket of his blazer. "Consider that last communication null and void as of this moment. Please, read this before you say anything else."

Daisy did as he asked. It was indeed brief and to the point—and mind-boggling in its scope. August was setting up a trust fund in Brianna's name. Daisy gasped; the amount of money was staggering. Brianna would be well taken care of for the rest of her life. But that wasn't all. He was making Daisy the sole administrator of the trust with a generous yearly stipend of her own. She looked up and found him watching her. "You aren't mentioned anywhere in the document. Four days ago you were going to try to prove I was an unfit mother and take my baby away from me. Today you are settling a fortune on her and by extension on me, and you want nothing in return?"

"You are mistaken. I want a great deal in return," he said candidly. "I want to be Brianna's grandfather."

"We want to be part of her life, to watch her grow up. To know her and love her," Fiona said, watching Brianna who was attempting, not very successfully, to follow the sound of their voices. Her little face puckered up. Her arms waved in the air. She began to whimper. Automatically Daisy turned and picked her up.

"I don't know," Daisy said, pressing the baby against her heart, swaying to and fro in the way mothers had soothed their babies, and themselves, since time began. "How do I know I can trust you?"

"You have my word," August said. "I may be a lot of things, including a poor excuse for a father and stepfather, but no one has ever accused me of going back on my word once I have given it." He held out his hand. His voice roughened. "For the sake of my son's memory and whatever place he still holds in your heart, believe me."

"He does have a place in my heart," Daisy whispered, and that was true even though she now wanted to look to the future and not the past. Brendan would always be the laughing, carefree boy she fell in love with. She was kind enough to think he would have matured into a good man, even if they were destined not to stay together. She held out her hand. "We have a deal."

CHAPTER THIRTEEN

QUINN LIFTED HIS HAND in salute as the security guard posted outside the VIP lot waved him through the gate. He was late. Daisy would be wondering where he was. Gil Sizemore was no pushover. He drove a hard bargain, but in the end Quinn was confident they would come to full agreement and Rev Energy Drinks' contract to sponsor Eli Ward and the No. 502 car would be extended for the foreseeable future. He couldn't wait to tell Daisy.

Hosting his regional sales reps and department heads tonight was his last obligation of the weekend. It would be a long evening factoring in the after-race celebration if—no, when—Eli Ward made the Chase. His driver was only twenty points out of contention and he'd qualified well. A top-ten finish would probably net him eleventh or twelfth. Still good enough to make the Chase, but a top-five finish would move him even higher in the standings. Eli had done what he'd asked of him back before the Bristol race. He was focused and steady and driving like a winner. Maybe his new girlfriend had something to do with that? Quinn could foresee a long, successful partnership for Rev and Eli and Double S Racing. But right now he had other, even more important partnerships on his mind.

After the race he would try to coax Daisy to return to the cabin for at least a few more days, long enough for him to convince her that was where she belonged—with him. The three of them together, a family. He didn't kid himself it would be easy. She was determined to show his stepfather and the world in general she could make it on her own; but he was just as stubborn as she was, and he had one big plus on his side. He was in love with her.

The electric motor of the golf cart was nearly silent. He could hear the public address announcer introducing the drivers and their teams. The opening ceremonies had already begun. If he didn't hurry they wouldn't get Brianna settled in with Juliana Grosso and make it to the suite before the green flag dropped.

He slid the golf cart into the small parking area alongside half a dozen others and took off for his leased motor home at a trot, but pulled up short when he saw his mother and stepfather standing beneath the awning that opened along the length of the motor home. Daisy seemed to be escorting them to their golf cart. Brianna was not with her mother.

His heart began to beat heavily in his chest. His plan hadn't worked. August had tracked them down before he was ready. Another forty-eight hours and he would have had it all nailed down. He knew once Daisy met with her attorney, Angela Merton, and realized how competent she was, she would relax and begin to think beyond the immediacy of protecting herself and Brianna from his stepfather by pulling up stakes and leaving Mooresville and the life she'd created for herself there.

Now that he had found her, she would be more determined than ever to escape August. She would cut herself off from not only her friends but from Quinn, himself, if that's what she thought it would take to keep her daughter safe.

The last untenable realization brought him to within an arm's length of his stepfather and his mother. "What are you doing here?" he asked, projecting the same icy calm August showed the world. He was good at it. He'd learned it from the master, himself.

"We came to speak to Miss Brookshire," August said,

looking down his patrician nose but oddly enough his expression was neither as aloof nor as studied as usual, and his mother was actually smiling. Daisy was smiling, too, although hers was more tentative as her eyes searched his face.

The smiles threw him off balance. "How did you find Daisy so quickly?" he demanded. He had never thought his scheme to hide her in plain sight was foolproof, but he had thought he knew August well enough that he had counted on the old man looking in the direction of Daisy's family in Florida first.

"It was your mother's idea," August said, nodding in Fiona's direction with a slight smile. "She said Daisy would stick with her friends, not run off to her parents and chance me turning my sights on them, too, and, as usual, she was right. Once I saw the sense in that it didn't take me long to track her down."

His mother's idea? August did not take advice from his wife. Not that Quinn recalled. "You're right," he growled. "Daisy has friends. Good friends who'll stand by her. Me included. And she has a lawyer, August, a good one. You'll never get a judge to declare Daisy an unfit mother." His hands had balled into fists. He had to stop himself from shaking one of them in the older man's face.

August held up his hands, palms out. "Slow down, son. I've already figured it out for myself—with your mother's help. I don't intend to make our family issues a public spectacle," he continued, glancing around the closely parked motor homes, although most of the occupants had already made their way out of the lot and into the suites and grandstand seats, "but maybe it's time you realized that just because your mother defers to my old-fashioned, chauvinist notions of how a wife behaves in public doesn't mean I don't value her counsel in private. You of all people should know how smart and savvy she is." August held out his hand. "I've made my peace with Daisy. I'm willing to make my peace with you for your mother's sake, if not our own."

Quinn had no idea what had transpired inside the motor home before he arrived but his mother's hopeful expression and radiant smile lowered the degree of tension inside him. "Please, Quinn," she whispered. "Let's try being a family again."

He couldn't deny her this small gesture of peace and goodwill. He had a lot of things to think about, a lot of old hurts and prejudices to take out and reconsider in light of what his stepfather had just said. He accepted August's handshake. "I'll do my best," he said and meant it.

"That's all I'm asking."

The strains of the National Anthem came over the loud-speakers. The opening ceremonies were nearing a conclusion. In another minute or two the command to "start your engines" would ring out and even here the noise would be deafening. "Your mother and I need to be going," August said. "We have to be at the heliport in thirty minutes."

"You're not staying for the race?" Daisy asked. It was the first she had spoken but there was a new lightness in her tone that Quinn hadn't heard before.

"I...um," August seemed at a loss for words. He was out of his element and it showed, but Quinn with his new perspective on their marriage wondered how long it would be before his mother got his stepfather interested in stock car racing. He would bet money now that Fiona and August would be in attendance when next season's racing kicked off at Daytona.

"Perhaps we'll come to one of the Chase races," Fiona inserted smoothly, "to cheer on the Rev Energy Drinks car."

"Yes," August said, "perhaps we will." Boy, when he was wrong, he was wrong in spades, Quinn decided.

From inside the motor home Brianna let out a lusty wail.

"She's hungry," Daisy said. "I need to feed her."

"We'll go." Fiona reached out and touched Quinn's sleeve. "Thank you, Quinn." She reached up and gave him a quick hug. "She let me hold the baby," she whispered in his ear, a catch in her voice. "Take care of her. Take care of both of them."

"WHAT DID YOUR MOTHER SAY to you?" Daisy asked as they watched the Carlyles drive away. She was shaking like a leaf with reaction but all in all she was proud of the way she'd handled herself. She only wished now that the confrontation was over that Quinn had been there. She had handled it on her own but she had missed his strong, comforting presence at her side.

She glanced at him from the corner of her eye and saw he was scowling at the rear of the retreating golf cart. He shifted his gaze to her face. "She said you let her hold Brianna. That was good of you."

She didn't think that was all Fiona had whispered in his ear but Brianna was still fussing in the salon so she didn't quiz him further. She turned and headed back inside, trusting that he would follow her up the steps. "It was the least I could do." She picked up the paper with the details of the trust August had proposed and handed it to him. She watched as he read the contents.

"This is a very generous trust," he said, choosing his words carefully.

"He really did love Brendan. I think he will grow to love Brianna, too. He cares for you, too, in his way."

"He's going to make you the sole administrator." Quinn ignored her last comment and she sighed inwardly. She hadn't thought it would be easy did she, reconciling two such forceful personalities?

"I think I'm going to have to go back to school and study

economics or financial planning or something," she said, hoping she could coax the frown from his face.

"You'll never have to go back to work at Cut 'N' Chat again if you don't want to, that's for sure." Quinn put the paper aside and bent to lift Brianna from her carrier, jiggling her up and down in his arms as though it was the most natural thing in the world for him to do. Her daughter quieted immediately, gazing up at Quinn with big, dark eyes.

Daisy took the paper from him and folded it carefully. "I never thought I could be a full-time mom. That's another thing I can thank your mother for making possible."

"Yeah, I have a hell of a lot of rethinking to do when it comes to my mom and August," he said, shaking his head.

"You and he may even become friends."

"I'm not sure that will ever happen, but I imagine we can be civil to each other from now on for my mom's sake."

"And Brianna's?" she asked, not quite brave enough to be more direct.

"The two of you don't need me anymore, Daisy. You have all the money you need."

"Having enough money is good but it's not everything."

Quinn took a step toward her. "Dammit, Daisy. I'm tired of tap dancing around the real issue between us. Do you want me around just for moral support because that's not going to be enough for me."

She looked into his eyes. She couldn't read his mind as he sometimes did hers. She didn't know what was in his thoughts or his heart. "I can take care of myself," she said. "I can take care of Brianna."

She saw the words hit him like a blow and oddly his despair gave her new courage. "Okay, I guess that answers my question."

"It doesn't answer mine," she said. "Are you offering to take care of us because you think it's what Brendan would want you to do? If it is, then the answer is no, I won't stay.

Not with you, not in Mooresville." She held her breath. She had just taken the biggest leap of faith in her life.

He didn't answer immediately but looked down at her daughter. "What do you say, Brianna?" he asked softly. "Do you want to move to Florida with your mommy just to prove how brave and strong and self-reliant two women on their own can be? Or do you want to stay here…the three of us together?" Brianna gave a little wiggle and shoved her fist in her mouth, cooing in his arms. Quinn looked at Daisy and the darkness had left his eyes and his smile, his wonderful smile, took her breath away. "I'm betting that means she isn't interested in moving to Florida just to prove a point. What about you, Daisy? Will you stay because I want you and need you…because I'm falling in love with you?"

Those words were what she'd wanted to hear. She didn't need to consider her answer for more than a handful of seconds. "Yes," she said, moving into the circle of his arms, placing her hand over his where it curled beneath Brianna's bottom. "Yes, I'll stay because I'm almost certain I'm falling in love with you, too."

Quinn bent his head and kissed her. When their lips met the earth moved beneath her feet and the roar of a thousand dragons filled her ears…or at least the roar of forty-three racing V-8s. "The race is starting," she said, breathless when he lifted his mouth from hers.

"Dammit, the race. Daisy—"

"I know, I know. We have to go."

"That was our first kiss but it sure as heck isn't going to be the last."

"I hope not," she said, laying her hand against his cheek, something she'd been yearning to do for days and days. "We have all the time in the world to make our plans for the future, Quinn."

"You're right," he said, grinning as he bent his head to

steal one more, quick kiss. "And we're going to start making those plans tonight."

Daisy smiled. "Just as soon as the Rev Energy Drinks car takes the checkered flag."

* * * * *

HARLEQUIN®

A Romance

FOR EVERY MOOD™

Spotlight on

Inspirational

Wholesome romances
that touch the heart and soul.

See the next page
to enjoy a sneak peek from
the Love Inspired® inspirational series.

CATINSPLI10

*See below for a sneak peek at
our inspirational line, Love Inspired®.
Introducing HIS HOLIDAY BRIDE
by bestselling author Jillian Hart*

Autumn Granger gave her horse rein to slide toward the town's new sheriff.

"Hey, there." The man in a brand-new Stetson, black T-shirt, jeans and riding boots held up a hand in greeting. He stepped away from his four-wheel drive with "Sheriff" in black on the doors and waded through the grasses. "I'm new around here."

"I'm Autumn Granger."

"Nice to meet you, Miss Granger. I'm Ford Sherman, from Chicago." He knuckled back his hat, revealing the most handsome face she'd ever seen. Big blue eyes contrasted with his sun-tanned complexion.

"I'm guessing you haven't seen much open land. Out here, you've got to keep an eye on cows or they're going to tear your vehicle apart."

"What?" He whipped around. Sure enough, mammoth black-and-white creatures had started to gnaw on his four-wheel drive. They clustered like a mob, mouths and tongues and teeth bent on destruction. One cow tried to pry the wiper off the windshield, another chewed on the side mirror. Several leaned through the open window, licking the seats.

"Move along, little dogie." He didn't know the first thing about cattle.

The entire herd swiveled their heads to study him curiously. Not a single hoof shifted. The animals soon returned to chewing, licking, digging through his possessions.

Autumn laughed, a warm and wonderful sound. "Thanks,

I needed that." She then pulled a bag from behind her saddle and waved it at the cows. "Look what I have, guys. Cookies."

Cows swung in her direction, and dozens of liquid brown eyes brightened with cookie hopes. As she circled the car, the cattle bounded after her. The earth shook with the force of their powerful hooves.

"Next time, you're on your own, city boy." She tipped her hat. The cowgirl stayed on his mind, the sweetest thing he had ever seen.

*Will Ford be able to stick it out in the country
to find out more about Autumn?
Find out in HIS HOLIDAY BRIDE
by bestselling author Jillian Hart,
available in October 2010
only from Love Inspired®.*

Copyright © 2010 by Jill Strickler

SHLIEXP1010

FROM #1 *NEW YORK TIMES*
AND *USA TODAY* BESTSELLING AUTHOR

DEBBIE MACOMBER

Mrs. Miracle on 34th Street…

This Christmas, Emily Merkle (just call her Mrs. Miracle)
is working in the toy department at Finley's, the last
family-owned department store in Manhattan.

Her boss (who happens to be the owner's son) has placed
an order for a large number of high-priced robots, which
he hopes will give the business a much-needed boost. In
fact, Jake Finley's counting on it.

Holly Larson is counting on that robot, too. She's been
looking after her eight-year-old nephew, Gabe, ever since
her widowed brother was deployed overseas. Holly plans
to buy Gabe a robot—which she can't afford—because
she's determined to make Christmas special.

But this Christmas will be different—thanks to Mrs.
Miracle. Next to bringing children joy, her favorite activity
is giving romance a nudge. Fortunately, Jake and Holly
are receptive to her "hints." And thanks to Mrs. Miracle,
Christmas takes on new meaning for Jake. For all of them!

Call Me Mrs. Miracle

Available wherever books are sold
September 28!

MIRA®

www.MIRABooks.com

MDM2819

Love Inspired
HISTORICAL
INSPIRATIONAL HISTORICAL ROMANCE

Fan favorite

VICTORIA BYLIN

takes you back in time to the Wyoming frontier
where life, love and faith were all tested.

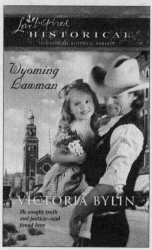

Wyoming Lawman

He sought truth and justice—
and found a family at the same time.

Available October wherever you buy books.

www.SteepleHill.com

Steeple
Hill®

LIH82846

HARLEQUIN®

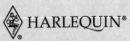

Texas Legacies: The McCabes

The McCabes of Texas are back!
5 new stories from popular author

CATHY GILLEN THACKER

The Triplets' First Thanksgiving
(October 2010)

Paige Chamberlain desperately wants to be a mother…
but helping former rival Kurt McCabe raise three
abandoned babies isn't quite what she had in mind.
There's going to be a full house at the McCabe
residence this holiday season!

Also watch for
A Cowboy under the Mistletoe *(December 2010)*

"LOVE, HOME & HAPPINESS"

www.eHarlequin.com

HAR75329

REQUEST YOUR
FREE BOOKS!

2 FREE NOVELS
FROM THE ROMANCE COLLECTION
PLUS 2 FREE GIFTS!

YES! Please send me 2 FREE novels from the Romance Collection and my 2 FREE gifts (gifts are worth about $10). After receiving them, if I don't wish to receive any more books, I can return the shipping statement marked "cancel." If I don't cancel, I will receive 4 brand-new novels every month and be billed just $5.74 per book in the U.S. or $6.24 per book in Canada. That's a saving of at least 28% off the cover price. It's quite a bargain! Shipping and handling is just 50¢ per book.* I understand that accepting the 2 free books and gifts places me under no obligation to buy anything. I can always return a shipment and cancel at any time. Even if I never buy another book, the two free books and gifts are mine to keep forever.

194/394 MDN E7NZ

Name	(PLEASE PRINT)

Address		Apt. #

City	State/Prov.	Zip/Postal Code

Signature (if under 18, a parent or guardian must sign)

Mail to **The Reader Service:**
IN U.S.A.: P.O. Box 1867, Buffalo, NY 14240-1867
IN CANADA: P.O. Box 609, Fort Erie, Ontario L2A 5X3

Not valid for current subscribers to the Romance Collection
or the Romance/Suspense Collection.

Want to try two free books from another line?
Call 1-800-873-8635 or visit www.morefreebooks.com.

* Terms and prices subject to change without notice. Prices do not include applicable taxes. N.Y. residents add applicable sales tax. Canadian residents will be charged applicable provincial taxes and GST. Offer not valid in Quebec. This offer is limited to one order per household. All orders subject to approval. Credit or debit balances in a customer's account(s) may be offset by any other outstanding balance owed by or to the customer. Please allow 4 to 6 weeks for delivery. Offer available while quantities last.

Your Privacy: Harlequin Books is committed to protecting your privacy. Our Privacy Policy is available online at www.eHarlequin.com or upon request from the Reader Service. From time to time we make our lists of customers available to reputable third parties who may have a product or service of interest to you. If you would prefer we not share your name and address, please check here. ☐

Help us get it right—We strive for accurate, respectful and relevant communications. To clarify or modify your communication preferences, visit us at www.ReaderService.com/consumerschoice.

MROM10R